# ACCIDENTAL SURPRISE

ANNIE J. ROSE

Photography: Wander Aguiar

# CHAPTER 1

## EMILY

I stared out the window at the dreary, gray sky. New York City in the spring, what a place to be. The thing was, though, that it was exactly where I wanted to be. I had grown up dreaming of the big city. The lights, the excitement, a city where there was always something happening.

Somehow, in the time that I'd been going to school there, I'd managed to carve a place for myself. New York City was mine.

Or so I'd always thought.

I sighed quietly as the train pulled away from the platform. Who knew when I would see the buildings again? If ever.

I tried not to think so darkly, but the truth was, I just had no idea what was going to happen with my future. My thoughts were in a whirl as I contemplated it. I used to have a clear vision for myself. I was going to go to school in New York City. I was going to intern at some of the top fashion houses in the world and make connections. With my degree under my belt, I was going to launch my own line with a little financial help from my parents.

It had all been going so well for me, that was the real kicker. It had all been going so well, until it wasn't.

The past month had been full of massive changes. Not things like a new internship in some exotic foreign country or anything good like that. These were *bad* changes. And not things like a terrible haircut, or even losing my scholarship through the school. I could have handled those.

The train slowed on its way into another station. Getting out of the city always took a little while. I wasn't sure if I wanted the train to never leave or if I wanted it to pick up speed so that I didn't have to linger in the place I had come to love.

Whatever happened, there was no going back.

I was just hoping that this trip home to Saratoga Springs would help me sort some things out. Unfortunately, I didn't hold out much hope for my current lifestyle. My one-bedroom Manhattan apartment was surely a thing of the past. My position in one of the most prestigious fashion design programs in the world would no doubt be another of the casualties, because there was no way that I could afford the tuition even with my scholarship.

There was no bank in the world that would agree to loan me anything, not in light of my father's mistake in trusting the wrong man.

I wished I could figure out how it had gotten to this point. I *thought* my father was a shrewd businessman and investor. Hadn't we all learned by now not to trust fraudsters? If only we could rewind time back to the point before my father had invested practically all of the family fortune into what had amounted to nothing more than a Ponzi scheme.

That was impossible, though. I wished that I could

make the best of the situation, but all of it was completely foreign to me.

My phone buzzed with a text from Alyssa. I supposed that was one good thing to come out of all of this mess. I hadn't seen nearly enough of my friends since I had been in New York. In spite of the scandal, they seemed ready to welcome me back home with open arms.

I hated that I was forced to go back home, but at least I'd get to spend some more time with all of them.

Alyssa wanted to know when I'd be getting in and if I'd like her to give me a ride to my parents' place. I knew she was offering because she felt sorry for me. She knew that I was used to private cars with chauffeurs who bent to my every whim. *This is just your chance to see how the rest of us live,* she had joked when I lamented about the trip home.

I had rolled my eyes at the message. Alyssa's family wasn't nearly as well-off as my family had always been, but they definitely did well enough for themselves.

I considered her offer now, though. I had planned on taking a taxi to my parents' mansion (or their former mansion, I supposed), but with everything so up in the air, I should probably be saving every dollar I had. I texted Alyssa back with my arrival time and thanked her for offering a ride.

Then I sat back, thinking about what awaited me at home.

I should quit thinking of it as 'home,' I knew. The ornate house that I had grown up in would never belong to my family again. There had been no choice but to sell it. In fact, that was the whole reason I was returning home now: to help my parents clear out whatever belongings they were keeping and move them from their mansion and into a small, two-bedroom condo. They would have just enough savings left that they would be able to live modestly through their retirement.

Nothing more than that.

I swallowed hard as I thought about it. I had never felt so on my own before. The Andrews family had always had money. It had been no skin off my parents' teeth to pay for my tuition or for the rent of my NYC apartment. That had all changed now, though.

When my parents first broke the news to me, I had been in shock and disbelief. Surely, they would somehow manage to recover their fortune. Surely things would turn around sooner than they thought. Losing everything was just the worst-case scenario, and they wanted to make sure that I was prepared for it just in case that was what happened.

Somewhere along the line, I realized that it wasn't just the worst-case scenario, though. It was reality. My parents had lost everything; there was no question about it. There was no getting that fortune back.

That was when my feelings had slipped more toward naïveté. It wasn't what I wanted, but surely, I could just simply get a job and keep my life mostly as it was. I'd wait tables or brew coffee, maybe bartend some evenings of the week. But I'd keep my apartment and keep on track in school, even if it meant I didn't have much of a social life anymore.

I think it was around the time of my third job interview that I realized there was no way that was happening either. I would be lucky to find someone who was willing to hire me, given my lack of experience and the fact that my family name was splattered all across the tabloids for everyone to read about. Even if I could find a job, I'd be lucky to scrape out enough to pay for the rent on my apartment, let alone everything else.

I thought about giving up my apartment. I could find a roommate and pay less in rent. If I did that and got a job, surely, I could continue my degree program, right? I wasn't far away from graduating.

But the only places I could afford to live were far out away from the school, and when I factored in the commute to and from my classes, I knew I could never get enough hours at a job to be able to pay for my tuition.

How did other students do it? It seemed impossible.

I stared down at the sketchpad in my lap. The page was blank, just waiting for my pencil to streak across it in bold lines. The rest of the book was full of sketches of fashion designs for the line that I had been hoping to launch.

I'd always loved fashion. It took me forever to be confident in my designs, but I had finally gotten there. Now I was on the cusp of starting the career that I had always dreamed about, but it looked like that dream was about to go up in smoke.

The foggy gray outside my window felt just as constricting as the rest of my situation at the moment.

I flipped the sketchbook closed, knowing that I wasn't going to be able to draw anything then. Or if I did, it wouldn't be anything that I'd want to show to anyone. There was just too much misery in my head. Misery didn't lend itself to couture.

It wasn't as though it was my first time returning to Saratoga Springs since I had moved to NYC, and technically, I still had a place back in Manhattan and a semester to finish out. But the trip home felt different. I was going to need to make some decisions, and I was dreading it.

What if I was going home to stay? Life in Saratoga would be a lot cheaper than life in NYC. There wasn't much of a fashion community there, but maybe fashion wasn't in the cards for me. I couldn't help feeling like I had passed on too many opportunities and burned too many bridges in my life, so sure that things were going to work out for me. But maybe they weren't meant to be.

I thought gloomily about the one person in particular who probably could have helped me out now. Not that he would have, given our history. In my mind's eye, I could picture him just as clearly as though I had seen him yesterday. Those piercing blue eyes, that crooked smile.

But no. I wasn't going to go there. I doubted Patrick was even in Saratoga at the moment. I wasn't the only one who had moved away. I pushed thoughts of him out of my mind and focused on the rain outside the window.

I was going to have to figure out some way to make it on my own, even if there was next to nothing on my résumé. Maybe I'd have to give up my fashion studies as well as my apartment, but I'd be able to make it somehow. I'd take an apartment with a couple of roommates and eke out a living doing something. I was going to stay in New York, though. Coming back to Saratoga for longer than it took to help my parents move was out of the question.

I had no doubt that it would be a time-consuming task, but it was one that I was ready for. I had always had an eye for detail and organization, after all. We'd get them all squared away in their new condo, and then I would start to figure out my own life.

*One thing at a time, Emily. Take it one thing at a time.*

# CHAPTER 2

## PATRICK

I wandered through Saratoga Springs. The place looked pretty much the same as I had left it. The quaint, historic downtown, the luxury spas, and the tourists crawling over the little boutiques and bistros. I hadn't been home in a few years, and there were a couple changes. Businesses that had been bought, new places that had sprung up. Overall, everything was about the same, though.

I couldn't say that I had missed the place, to be honest. There were plenty of things that I would always love about Saratoga, but there had also been plenty of reasons to leave.

One major reason, really. A reason with stunning blue eyes and a body that would be burned into my memory for the rest of my life.

For the billionth time, I blocked those memories from my consciousness. It was bad enough that I had to keep reliving them, or some variation of them, in my dreams. I didn't need to be thinking about them every waking moment as well.

Of course, it was easier to forget about her when I wasn't in Saratoga Springs, and when I wasn't pacing back and forth outside an upscale restaurant, waiting for my business partner and best friend to arrive for dinner. Even though the restaurant was only a few blocks from the luxury hotel that we were staying at, Jonah was taking his sweet time arriving.

I glanced at my watch and frowned. I had plenty of things that I could be doing right then besides attending a dinner meeting with the magazine folks. Their idea for the photo shoot was idiotic anyway, if you asked my opinion.

Jonah thought it would be good for publicity. I kept trying to remind him that the business was doing absurdly well on its own, without having photos of me touted in every magazine in the country. Jonah always reminded me that my good looks weren't going to last forever and that I'd better flaunt them while I still could.

I knew he was just looking out for me, and I appreciated his concern. He wanted to see me happy long-term, and not just because of business successes. But a magazine spread wasn't the way to go about that.

Especially not when magazine people were *always* late.

Finally, Jonah arrived with the guys in tow. "You could have headed inside without us," one of them said.

I shrugged and glanced at Jonah, who gave me an apologetic look. What Alex and the other magazine guys didn't realize was that not only was this my hometown, but I knew pretty much everyone here. If I had headed inside on my own, I would have had to make small talk with people who'd barely paid any attention to me when I was younger, who now all wanted to know how my business was going.

I wasn't stupid. No one in this town had ever expected me to make anything of myself. Well, look at me now.

We headed inside and were seated at the table that Jonah had reserved for us. We ordered drinks first, and then

Alex launched into a discussion about the magazine spread. "I know you probably don't think that your business's target audience has much overlap with our magazine's readership," he said, giving a rueful laugh. "But we're always interested in young entrepreneurs like yourself, regardless of the industry that you're in. You've made quite a name for yourself, first with sports and then with business."

The man laughed, and I tried not to grimace. He made it sound like the whole thing had been so easy. That grated on me, but then again, it was nothing unusual. Unfortunately, it was easier for them all to think that my opportunities had been somehow handed to me. Otherwise, they might realize that they too could have worked just as hard to become billionaires.

"So, we're thinking we're mainly going to do a photo shoot, and then add in some context in short-form," Alex continued. "Matt here is a photographer, and he's got some ideas for you."

"Yeah!" Matt broke in, flashing a smile at me. "So, I was thinking..." He droned on about the ideas that he had. To be honest, I was only half listening, absentmindedly stirring my old-fashioned as I watched various people come into the restaurant. Of course, they were mostly tourists, just there for the springs and relaxation.

There was a part of me that knew that I was looking for *her*, though. What if she were to walk in with her family? Or worse, with a boyfriend? A fiancé? Was there a possibility that she was engaged? Or married? I wanted to think that I would have heard if she was, but then again, I had been avoiding this place as much as I could for the past few years.

Matt finally ran out of ideas. I thought everything that he had proposed sounded pretty stupid, but then, the whole photo shoot wasn't the kind of thing that I wanted to do. Jonah was eating it all up, though. He looked nearly as excited as the photographer.

I tried not to sigh as I looked over at my business partner. "Not to be an ass, but are we sure that this sort of thing is the direction we want to take?" I asked him bluntly, unable to help myself. I knew that I should probably play nice in front of the magazine boys, but I was starting to feel a headache coming on, and the last thing I wanted to do was spend any more time in Saratoga than I had to.

From the sounds of it, though, Matt had at least fifteen different locations that he wanted me at, and between transport to locations and getting the lighting right, I had a feeling we could be here for a while.

Jonah gave me a look, and I could tell he was telling me to take it easy. "You're the face of the business," he reminded me, grinning at the other two men as though to let them in on the joke. "You've got to make the right impression. You know, really get people talking."

I raised an eyebrow. "And the right impression involves dressing me up like an oversized jockey at the racetrack?" Were they even going to be able to find a jockey outfit that fit my height and stature?

"I know it sounds a bit farfetched," Alex immediately broke in. "It's a metaphor for the business world, though. You see?" And he was off, prattling nearly as much as Matt had when he'd first introduced the idea.

Metaphors were all well and good, but it still seemed pretty over the top if you asked me. Jonah was nodding along again, though, and I knew that whatever outfits they wanted, I was going to be dressed up in them. Whatever. I would play pretend for the sake of the brand, but that didn't mean I was buying the bullshit they were selling to the general public.

Fortunately, once the initial conversation about the magazine spread was done, with Jonah's okay and my tacit approval on everything, we quit talking shop and got to enjoy our meal. I had to admit, I would much rather spend the evening at the diner, just like old times, but this wasn't bad either.

The dinner meeting finally wrapped up, and Jonah and I grabbed our coats and headed back toward his hotel.

"You all right, man?" Jonah asked when it was just the two of us. "You seem a little, I don't know, on edge. You were grumpy all night."

"Sorry," I said, knowing that I owed him an apology for my curt behavior when it came to the magazine folks. He had worked hard to set all of it up.

Jonah waved away the apology. "Seriously, don't worry about it," he said. "Just, what's up?"

I grimaced. "I'm not really a huge fan of my hometown," I admitted. "I grew up poor in a town full of mostly well-to-do folks. And I went to school with kids who would never let me forget it either."

"Yeah, fair enough," Jonah said. "It was the magazine's idea to bring you here. Something about 'getting to know the essence of you.'" From the way he said it, I could tell that not only was that a direct quote from one of the guys, but he was trying not to laugh at the wording.

I grinned crookedly and shoved my hands deeper into the pockets of my jacket. "It's fine, it just brings back some uncomfortable memories. But we'll get the photo shoot done, and I'll make sure to give the magazine some good quotes that show them, what was it, 'the essence of me.'" We both snorted at that.

The whole thing still seemed kind of hokey to me, but I would do no less where the business was concerned. For all of my resistance, I trusted Jonah. If he thought this was the way to get us more business, then it was what I would do.

"Promise I'll try to make things as quick and painless as possible," Jonah said.

I laughed. "As long as they still plan to dress me up as a jockey, or whatever other ridiculous idea they come up with, it's not going to be painless, I can tell you that right now."

"Who knows?" Jonah teased. "Maybe it'll raise your reputation with the ladies."

"Never had a problem in that department before," I said wryly.

"Guess not," Jonah agreed. "Although I can't say that I've ever seen you be particularly interested in any of the beauties throwing themselves at you."

I shrugged. For just a moment, I thought I saw a familiar-looking face up ahead of me, blue eyes peering at me through the dim light of the evening. I resisted the urge to snort at my own foolishness. There was far from just one blue-eyed female in this world. Even in a world narrowed down to Saratoga Springs.

Jonah was my best friend, but he didn't know everything about me, and he certainly didn't know about Emily and me, nor was I about to tell him. I just wasn't inclined to share that part of my past with anyone. There was still a lot of pain and resentment related to that first foray into romance, and I kept those feelings locked away where they couldn't distract me.

Besides, it wasn't like talking about it would ever amount to anything. Nothing that I or anyone else could do would ever make things right between Emily and me again.

No point in digging out all those feelings that I had once imagined I had for her.

"You want to get a drink at the hotel bar?" Jonah asked as we arrived at the lobby. Although he said it casually enough, I could tell from his eyes that he was wondering about some of the unspoken things from that evening.

I didn't want to talk about any of it, though, and I definitely didn't want to think about the photo shoot for another minute. "Think I'm just going to head home for the night," I told him.

Thankfully, Jonah and I had been friends for long enough that even though I knew he was curious about the details, he let me off the hook with just a nod. He clapped me on the shoulder. "See you in the morning for the first part of the photo shoot," he said. "Don't work too late tonight. Gotta get that beauty sleep."

I rolled my eyes, but I couldn't help grinning at him. It was a relief to go to my place and shut the door behind me. To shut out the rest of Saratoga. Not much had changed since the last time I'd been there. Things still hurt just the same.

## CHAPTER 3

### EMILY

I laughed as Elliot came to a stop while the light was still yellow. "You drive like a grandma now," I teased him.

He turned around and stuck his tongue out at me. "Last thing I need is another mark on my license," he said, shrugging. "Anyway, I'm not sixteen anymore."

"No, you certainly aren't," I said, unable to keep from eyeing what I could see of him.

I had been surprised to walk out of the train station to find Elliot standing there beside Alyssa. It was his shiny blue sports car that we got into as well. It wasn't like I was avoiding anyone from town, though. I hadn't seen Elliot in years, but he had been a friend since we were kids.

Alyssa leaned around her seat so that she could see me, where I was sitting in the back. "It is so good to see you," she said enthusiastically. "Honestly, we were all starting to think that you were never coming back."

"I've been back a few times," I protested, hating the defensive note that crept into my voice. It was the truth, though.

Alyssa rolled her eyes. "It's always around the holidays,

and everyone is always busy with family things," she reminded me. "This is different."

There was a silence in the car, and I could see Alyssa grimace a little as she realized what she had just said. Yes, things were certainly different this time around.

Fortunately, Elliot broke the silence. "Yeah, things are different," he said, his eyes meeting mine in the rearview mirror. "Can you believe we finally have a decent burrito shop in town?"

"Oh wow," I said dryly. "Things really have changed."

Alyssa laughed. "Well, not all that much has changed. There are a bunch of people around that we should get together with while you're here. Josh and Ingrid. Max. Let's see, who else? I think Molly and her brother, maybe? Molly just had a baby; can you believe it? Like, it's so weird to think that people our age are already getting married and buying houses and stuff. Let alone having kids."

I shrugged in the back seat and stared out the window. She made it sound like I was just home for a social visit. Like it was nothing more than that. "I don't know how much time I'll have," I reminded her, trying not to sound too sharp. "I'm going to be busy helping my parents pack up their house. And I might not be in the mood to hang out with everyone anyway."

"Oh, girl," Alyssa sighed, giving me a sympathetic look. "I'm so sorry that all of this is happening to you, you know? Like, what a mess." It didn't sound like she was being entirely genuine. I'd always been better off than her, and I knew that she had been at least a little jealous.

Not that her own position had ever been anywhere near as uncomfortable as mine currently was.

"Yeah, I'm sorry too," Elliot added, and I gave him a small smile, knowing that he, at least, was sincere. He'd always been a good friend, even if he had always been too obsessed with Alyssa for his own good. Alyssa kept him firmly in the friend-zone, but that hadn't stopped him from pining for her.

In fact, I thought gloomily, that was probably the only reason that he had agreed to pick me up from the station: so that he would have a reason to spend a little time with her. He wasn't there just to see me.

I pushed those thoughts aside and tried to focus on Alyssa as she filled me in on the town gossip. I could feel a headache coming on.

I hadn't been avoiding the place, necessarily. I had just gotten so caught up in school and everything else in NYC that I was out of the loop. To be honest, the more Alyssa babbled about the people that we had gone to school with, the more I realized that I didn't really care about all their petty small-town drama. I wasn't about to say that to her, though.

This was her whole world. She had never left. It would be mean for me to tell her that I didn't give a shit about any of it. Besides, hadn't I learned my lesson about burning my bridges? I needed all the friends I could get at the moment.

Finally, we arrived. Was it just me or was the house sagging under the weight of misery? No, probably just me. I put on a brave smile. "Thanks again for the ride," I told Elliot. "Good to see you guys."

"Hey, there's some sort of hang-out going on tonight at Carson's place," Alyssa said brightly. "If you want, we could come pick you up."

"That's okay," I said. "I should probably be with my family tonight. You know, my first night back and all." Again, I wasn't about to tell her that a 'hang-out,' probably in some guy's basement, wasn't exactly my speed anymore.

I missed the city already.

"Oh, right!" Alyssa said, not sounding fazed. "Well, I'll text you tomorrow and we can figure something out."

"If I have time," I reminded her.

"Of course, only if you have time," Alyssa said. Finally, she sounded like she was getting the message. I could tell that she wasn't happy, but oh well. I wasn't particularly happy at the moment either. She turned back to Elliot. "All right, take me into town. I want dinner."

I shook my head as they drove off. I remembered when I used to behave a lot more like Alyssa. I liked to think that I had become more self-aware in the last few years, especially now. With my family's reputation down the drain along with our funds, the only thing I was entitled to was trying to cope with my reversal in fortune.

I stood outside the mansion for a few moments, drinking in the sight of the place. What if it was the last time that I ever stood there? I had always thought that the place was kind of big for just our small family, but at the same time, it had always been home. I had never felt as attached to the place as I did now, seeing the 'For Sale' sign on the front lawn.

I frowned, surprised as childhood memories flooded my brain. I had learned to ride a bike over there. I had gotten my first kiss on that porch swing. So many other milestones had happened here. I found myself blinking back tears as I walked toward the front door.

If I was upset about it, I could only imagine how my parents must feel. This was their whole life, everything that they had ever worked for. It was the house that they had chosen, just after their marriage, as a place in which to raise their future family. The family that they were only just beginning to imagine.

Now, that whole dream was crumbling to dust. They were moving into a tiny condo, and everything that they had worked for was no more.

Sure enough, when I got inside, Mom immediately wrapped me in a big hug. It was one of those hugs that you could tell was more for her than for me. For several long minutes, she held on to me, and I could feel her body shaking with suppressed sobs. It wasn't long before Dad appeared in the hall as well. He absently patted Mom on the back, but there was something in his expression that told me that he wasn't really there in the moment.

I could only imagine how he must feel right then. Like it was all his fault, like he had let his family down. I wished that there was something that I could say to make him feel better, but I knew that he would probably just keep beating himself up over it anyway. And besides, I still couldn't believe that he had trusted everything that the family had to some guy who turned out to be a total scammer.

Maybe it was naïve, but I had just always thought that my father was smarter than that.

It felt like when you really become an adult and you realize that your parents aren't the heroes that you made them out to be when you were a kid. That they were just people like you, with all the same hurdles and dramas and whatever else. Only not only had I realized that my father was merely mortal, I had learned just how fallible he was.

How did you come back from something like that?

A pall of misery descended there in the hall as I hugged Mom and I wondered how we were ever going to make it through this.

# CHAPTER 4

## PATRICK

I continued to stare at the spreadsheet in front of me, but I knew that I wasn't giving it half of the attention that it deserved. Instead, my mind kept wandering. Being back in my hometown left me feeling slightly unsettled, and even though I was trying to avoid thinking about the reason for that, I just couldn't.

I'd left Saratoga Springs for a reason. I'd left this town with a broken heart.

I'd been lying to myself in the years that I'd been away, telling myself that I had healed. Now, though, I was starting to recognize those lies for what they were.

I hadn't healed. There was a reason that, as Jonah had pointed out, I wasn't interested in any of the women who threw themselves at me. There were plenty of attractive women in the bunch, of course. And I wasn't a monk. I had gone on some dates and taken some ladies to bed.

But I had never even considered having a serious relationship.

There were a number of reasons for that, I told myself. First of all, those women all made it too easy for me. I understood that I was attractive and that my wealth was a draw for them, but when they were practically throwing themselves at me, it just made me feel uncomfortable.

Besides, I was busy with my career. First, it had been the challenges of being a professional athlete. Between my training schedule and the travel schedule, it had been impossible to consider starting a serious relationship. Then I had started an outdoor retail company, and that took all of my focus.

Deep down, I knew those were simply excuses. There were plenty of athletes who had serious relationships. Families, even. And plenty of businessmen with the same. If I had wanted a relationship, I could have found the time.

The truth was that I didn't want one. Or rather, I wanted one, but with a specific person.

Those azure eyes flickered through my brain again.

I had been madly in love with her once, back in high school. She'd been a spoiled little rich girl, and we'd both been so young. But I would have done anything to have her. I could see the woman that she would one day become. She was determined and smart, and she knew what she wanted out of life. I had always admired that.

When we were together, just the two of us, things had been almost as perfect as they could get. I knew that we were young. I knew all the statistics about how high school relationships never really worked out. We would, though. I was sure of it. We were on the same page; we wanted the same things out of life. We fit so well together that neither of us could imagine our lives in any other way. Or so I had thought.

On the night of our high school graduation, I learned the truth.

We had been lying there in the back of my rusty old pickup truck, staring up at the stars. Emily was there in my arms, snuggled against my chest.

I pulled the blanket up over her shoulders, lightly kissing her hair and smiling contentedly. "So I got that hockey scholarship," I told her. I had been holding in the news all day long, wanting to enjoy our graduation before we started thinking about the future. But I knew she would be just as excited as I was.

"What?" Emily asked in surprise, craning her neck to look up at me. "You've been hiding that from me all day? That's amazing, Pat!"

"Yeah," I said, grinning at her. I held her a little closer. "So, I was thinking, now that we're both going to the same school next year, maybe we could move in together. I know you really want to do the dorms, but I've been looking into Marsh Hall and they have ones for couples. We could start off there for our freshman year, and then we can move off campus and get our own place."

I phrased things tentatively, but I was sure that she would say yes. That was why we had applied to some of the same schools, after all: so that we could figure out a way to keep this thing going. Neither of us really wanted to do the distance thing. Now we didn't have to.

But Emily kept staring up at the stars, not answering right away.

"I know it's a big step," I said, wondering if I had somehow misread what point we were at in our relationship. Or maybe she just wanted to go to one of the other schools that she had been accepted into. I hated the thought of that, but I was so damned proud of her for getting into such amazing schools that I knew I couldn't hold her back on my account. Besides, even if she went to NYC and I was still in upstate New York, it wasn't that long of a commute. I could drive down and see her every weekend.

Emily was still quiet. "What's wrong?" I finally asked her.

"I've decided that I'm not going to school next year," she finally admitted.

"What?" I asked in shock. "You're just going to stay here? And do what?"

I didn't mean to sound so appalled at the idea, but I just couldn't picture her here. There were plenty of people from our high school who would be sticking around, but I had never imagined Emily to be one of them. She had too much potential for that.

"Not staying in Saratoga, no," Emily said, shifting uncomfortably away from me. "I was planning on taking a gap year to travel Europe before I decide on a school."

I stared down at her as though she had grown two heads. A gap year? In Europe? So much for not doing the distance thing. Unless she meant that she wanted both of us to go? We had talked about our future in the past, or at least I had talked about it. I suddenly realized that she had never really told me what her plans were.

Still, she could have at least mentioned the Europe thing at some point. I had been saving up money working at the hardware store all year, but I would have saved more if I knew that there was a big European adventure on the horizon.

"Europe, okay," I said, blowing out a breath through my nose. "Where do we start? Have you booked flights for us already?"

Emily looked pained. "Pat, I really think this is something that I need to do on my own," she finally said.

I stared at her. Something that she needed to do on her

own? Here I was, unable to imagine a life without her, and she thought that this was something she needed to do on her own?

"Come on," she said, sitting up and pulling her knees up to her chest. She gave a bitter laugh, shaking her head. "We're just high school kids. From very different backgrounds. Did you really expect this to last forever?"

I felt like I could barely breathe. It was as though she had ripped my heart right out of my chest and crushed it in her hand. Before I could say anything, she hopped out of the truck, waving over her shoulder as she had a million times before.

But as I watched her walk back toward town, I knew that this time she was leaving me for good.

I PRESSED my fingertips against my eyeballs as I willed the memories away. I hadn't been the same since that night.

It had been productive in a way. I had channeled all of that heartbreak and disappointment into hockey. I managed to put together some solid grades my freshman year of college, and more than that, I'd managed to carve out a place for myself on the school team. By the time I graduated, it was only a matter of course that I would go pro.

I barely remembered the hit that had ended my career. There was a lot of anger and frustration after that. I came back home for a while, long enough to realize that there was nothing for me there. Finally, I had put that business degree to good use, channeling all that continued heartache into building an empire.

I was a massive success now. The magazine spread was only the latest in a string of things that reminded me that I wasn't just some heartbroken teenager anymore. Sometimes, though, I still felt like that young and stupid eighteen-year-old.

I ran a hand through my hair and leaned back in my chair, trying to clear my head. Jonah had said that we would get through the photo shoot and interview as quickly as possible. Then I'd get the hell out of Saratoga Springs again.

*And I won't return anytime soon,* I promised myself. *Or ever.*

# CHAPTER 5

## EMILY

Dinner with my parents could not have been more awkward. Mom still looked like she was on the verge of tears. Dad ate his food as though he was a robot, just shoveling it in like he couldn't even taste it. Nobody said a single thing.

As for me, I wasn't hungry. I should have been, but my appetite seemed to have fled ever since I got the call telling me that my parents would be selling the house.

There was a certain heaviness that had descended on the place that made everything feel so damned uncomfortable. There we were, the three of us. I pushed food around on my plate, unable to take a single bite. Mom dabbed at her eyes with her napkin to dry her tears. Dad was staring off into space, as though all the answers to the universe were somewhere just beyond what he could see.

We had been happy, once upon a time. The real American family, living out the real American dream. Dad, a successful businessman; Mom, the perfect wife and mother; me, the aspiring fashion designer who traveled the world taking internships in beautiful places.

No more.

Finally, I couldn't take the tragic atmosphere for another minute. "Excuse me," I said, standing up quickly enough that my chair scraped noisily across the floor. Both my parents looked up at me. I could feel myself blush. "I'm kind of tired. I think I'm going to head upstairs and try to pack up some of my room, then head to bed."

"Sure, sweetie," Mom said distantly. She dabbed at her eyes again, probably thinking about how this was probably the final meal that we would share here in this house, at this table, all three of us.

I hurried off before I could think too long and hard about that. The last thing we needed was for me to start crying as well. Mom had cried more than enough for both of us already, and I hadn't even been there for a full day.

Upstairs in my old bedroom, I let out a sigh as I looked around. Nothing had changed since high school. There were years of memories that I was going to have to sort through, deciding what to keep and what to throw away or sell. The second bedroom in my parents' new condo would be a guest bedroom. Even if it had been mine, I had too much stuff in this spacious room to move into that other, much smaller place.

"This is a good thing," I told myself for the umpteenth time. "This is just a chance to get rid of things that I don't need or want anymore."

There had to be plenty of things that I didn't need or want anymore, after all. I had barely been back to the room in the ten years since I had graduated from high school, between my travel and my internships and my college schedule. If I hadn't needed any of this in all that time, then clearly none of it was very important.

If I was lucky, I'd be able to have everything I wanted to

keep boxed up in a matter of hours, and then I'd be able to help my parents start on the rest of the house. There would be a moving truck coming by later in the week to do the actual moving part, but in light of our current finances, it had seemed to make the most sense if we did the boxing ourselves, as well as moving the important things over.

I went over to the desk first, figuring those drawers were an easy enough place to start. They were probably full of pencils and gum wrappers, nothing that I needed to keep and nothing that I needed to reminisce about.

There wasn't a lot of time to reminisce. I had to keep reminding myself of that.

I made it through two of the drawers in no time, throwing most of the contents into the trash bag that I started. But as I pulled out the center drawer, I swallowed hard. There was Patrick's face, smiling up at me.

I gingerly picked up the picture, as though it might crumble into dust in my hand -- just like everything else these days.

It had always been one of my favorite pictures of him. He had that big, goofy smile on his face as he leaned back against the boards at our local ice rink. I had never been nearly as good at skating as he was, of course, but somehow, he had always made it so fun. And I liked seeing him out there on the ice. You could tell it was exactly where he belonged.

I dropped the picture as though it had burned me, but when it fluttered down to rest on the desk, his blue eyes were still staring up at me. There was no blame there; that was the only thing that reminded me that the picture was from way back in the past.

There would be accusation there now, I was sure. I absently rubbed at my finger, flinching when I didn't encounter the promise ring that he had proudly given me back in school. Fidgeting with that was a habit I'd thought I had long since trained out of myself. But of course, I was thinking about Patrick right now. It was only natural that I'd revert to old habits.

I shook my head. Pat. I hadn't thought about him this much in years. I hadn't let myself. My chest ached when I thought about him. He was the first man that I had ever loved, the one who took my virginity and my heart. But things hadn't ended well.

My eyes trailed across the photo of him at the rink again. That was where he had first asked me out, actually.

THAT DAY, I tugged at the laces on my skates, loosening them and sliding my feet out. *Brr.* I shivered as the cool air of the rink assaulted my socked feet. Quickly, I slid into my boots, lacing them up. When I looked up, I happened to glance over at the local hockey team that was just about to start practicing. They were having a meeting outside the boards as everyone from Laura's birthday party trickled off the ice.

I was surprised to see one of the guys staring at me. He had a big 'C' on the shoulder of his jersey, and there was something familiar about him. I probably knew him from around school; he looked like he was about my age. But with that helmet obscuring his looks, it was anyone's guess who he was.

I stood up and grabbed my skates. Who had their birthday party at the ice rink anymore anyway? What were we, five? I wouldn't have gone except that Laura's mom always hired the best caterers and didn't mind if she caught us sneaking wine. The after-party was going to be great.

With my skates off, I headed for the door to the lobby of the rink. But just as I was reaching for the handle, someone caught my wrist. "Hey." It was the guy from before, the captain of the hockey team.

I looked up into those blue eyes of his and suddenly realized that I knew who he was. Patrick.

I felt a faint blush on my face. He was one of the most popular jocks in the school. We didn't run in the same circles, but I definitely knew who he was. "I didn't realize you were the captain," I said, nodding towards the 'C' on his jersey.

He beamed at me. "New promotion," he said.

"Congrats," I said, glancing past him. The rest of the team was heading onto the ice. Why wasn't he following them?

"You're Emily Andrews, right?" he asked.

"Yeah," I said, immediately suspicious. What did he want?

Patrick jerked his head toward the rink. "I saw you out there. You're pretty good."

I shrugged. "Not really," I said. "I mean, I can get around on the ice; I grew up skating just like everyone else around here. But I'm not good."

"I think you are," Patrick said simply. He paused. "Anyway, I was just wondering if maybe you wanted to hang out sometime."

"And do what?" I asked blankly.

Patrick shrugged, grinning at me. "Anything," he said.

But just then, his coach blew his whistle, the shrill sound echoing through the rink. "Manning! Get your butt on the ice before I rip the 'C' off your jersey myself!"

"Oops, got to run," Patrick said, heading for the door.

"Skate," I corrected automatically. He paused for one

more second, looking quizzically back over his shoulder. "You've got to skate. Not run."

Patrick laughed at the lame joke. "Yeah, guess so," he said, his eyes twinkling with mirth. I liked his laugh, I decided. I liked the fact that I had *caused* him to laugh. "See you around, Emily."

Of course, I hadn't agreed to actually hang out with him, nor had I intended to. But that hadn't stopped him from sticking a sunflower in my locker every day for the rest of the week.

"Why sunflowers anyway?" I finally asked him.

"Because you like them. Don't you?" he asked. There was a crease between his brows, like he was actually worried about my answer. For a moment, I thought about fucking with him. Telling him that I hated sunflowers. But the four flowers were at home on my desk in a red vase, and every morning that week, I had smiled just looking at them.

"They're my favorite," I admitted. "How did you know that?"

"You drew that sunflower field in art class last year. The one that was hanging in the school exhibition," he said simply. "They were great."

I stared at him. "So what, you're like a stalker or something?" I asked weakly, wishing the words could come out more teasing. I had slaved over that picture for ages, and I'd barely gotten any sort of comment about it from the art teacher. Sure, it had hung in the exhibition, but half the class had gotten something accepted into that. It wasn't like it was anything special.

I still had a hard time feeling confident enough to show my work off like that. So, the fact that he had seen it and liked it? That made butterflies jump in my belly. I tried to quell the feeling.

Patrick grinned crookedly at me, leaning against the lockers. "Stalker? Only if you want me to be." He paused. "Have you given any thought to what I said at the rink? About hanging out sometime?"

I heard a noise of surprise off to my right. Alyssa, I was sure. God, this was so embarrassing. It was one thing for him to ask me out at the rink, but here at school, where anyone could hear? We were from two different worlds. And even though he was a popular athlete, he was still from the poorer section of town and not accepted as 'one of us.' There was no way that this could work.

"Why should I date you?" I asked him haughtily, tossing my hair.

Patrick stared at me for a long moment, his grin widening. He leaned in closer to me, his breath warm against the shell of my ear. I could smell the faintest hint of spicy cologne, and I thought my heart would stop right then.

"Let's just say, if you agree to go out with me, it'll be an adventure," he murmured. "I bet you could use an adventure in your life. Couldn't you, Emily?" He practically purred my name, and it was all that I could do not to melt into a puddle on the floor. Then he pulled back, grinning at me one more time before he sauntered away.

"What the hell was that about?" Alyssa asked, marching over to me.

I shook my head, my whole body buzzing with interest. "I have no idea," I said weakly.

He had been true to his word. It certainly had been an adventure. Not one that I wanted to think about now, though. I forced those memories to the back of my mind before I could get lost in what could have been.

I hastily swept that photo back into the drawer and turned away from my desk. Maybe the closet was a better place to start. There had to be some clothes in there that I could get rid of. My teenage self had tried her hardest to be stylish, but she was still developing her fashion sense.

As I stared into my closet, it seemed like all I could see were outfits that I had worn when Patrick and I were dating. I quickly shut the doors and grabbed my phone. Maybe I just needed to get out of the house for some air.

I texted Alyssa to see if she wanted to grab a drink. *Not at Carson's*, I clarified.

Her response was quick. *Haha, great. This place is lame. Pick you up in ten.*

I let out a breath that I hadn't realized I'd been holding. It was only overwhelming because everything was so up in the air at the moment. But I would never regret having left behind Patrick and Saratoga Springs and all of the rest of it. I refused to regret that.

# CHAPTER 6

## PATRICK

I finally closed my laptop, rubbing at my eyes. Then I stood up, feeling disconcerted. I had barely gotten any work done. It seemed like it should be later than it was. I couldn't go to sleep yet. I wasn't even remotely tired.

I walked over to the window and stared out over the town. Suddenly, my penthouse felt claustrophobic. I couldn't seem to get away from my thoughts. I knew that I should have taken Jonah up on his offer for a drink. Except that, then again, I hadn't felt like talking about everything. Jonah was a little too perceptive sometimes and I knew that he would get the full story out of me.

Still, I didn't feel like staying alone in my place right then either. I grabbed my keys and shoved them into my pocket. Then I grabbed my jacket. I just needed to get some fresh air. A little walk around downtown would do me good. Or at least, it wouldn't make me think about anything that I wasn't already thinking about.

Unsurprisingly, there were still plenty of people out on a Friday night, either wandering the streets, sitting down to a late dinner, or otherwise heading out on the town. I wandered past one of the oldest bars in the area. The doors were flung wide open to the cool spring air, and I could hear the music pulsing within.

I remembered the bar from before. The old building looked like it had been there since the time of the original settlers. It had always been a bit of a dive, but that had only given it a reputation among the well-to-do of the town as a place to "slum it" with everyone else. The place was pretty busy given that it was a Friday night. I scanned the crowd through the window, wondering if I would see anyone that I recognized.

I froze when I saw *her* in there. Emily. The very same girl that I couldn't get off my mind tonight.

I shook my head, sure that I was imagining things. Maybe I only thought that I saw her because I couldn't stop thinking about her. It was probably just some tourist who bore a passing resemblance to her. But when I looked again, I was sure that it was her. She was standing at the bar in a simple red sweater-dress and thigh-high boots, and she looked more amazing than ever.

I swallowed hard, my eyes tracing every inch of her curves as if to memorize them. As if she wasn't permanently etched into my memory already.

I thought about going inside. My first love, someone that I hadn't seen since high school graduation, was standing there in Saratoga Springs, mere feet from me. I could walk inside, take her into my arms, kiss her until she was breathless, and we were both aching with want.

But I wouldn't. I told myself to just keep walking. We had said all that we needed to say to each other years ago. There was no point in reopening old wounds. *Keep walk-*

*ing. Forget about her.* It was the sensible thing to do. The only thing that I could do, really.

But my feet didn't seem to be attached to my brain. Instead of continuing on down the street, I found myself walking into the bar. I didn't go straight over to her, though. Instead, I flagged down the bartender, as if I was just in here for a drink like everyone else.

While I was waiting for the bartender, someone appeared next to me, blocking my view of Emily. I looked at the man, surprised to see that it was Elliot. I knew him from back in school, although he had been more Emily's friend than mine.

He smiled warmly at me now. "Hey, man. Long time no see."

"Yeah," I said, shaking his hand. We'd run in different circles, but he'd always been a nice dude. Maybe too nice of a dude. He always let the girls walk all over him.

Elliot looked like he was about to say something, but before he could, there was a squeal of excitement. The next thing I knew, a woman had thrown herself into my arms. I hissed in pain as I stumbled to the side and bashed my ribs against the edge of the bar, but I managed to keep us both upright. For a moment, all I could see was blond hair. Then I recognized her: Alyssa, another one of Emily's friends. I tried not to recoil. Alyssa had always looked at me like she was hungry for something that I was keeping from her. It appeared that her interest in me hadn't changed in the years since I'd last seen her.

I set her away from myself. "Hi, Alyssa," I said, trying to be polite while also keeping my tone cool so that she would hopefully realize that I still wasn't interested.

My eyes slid past her, to where Emily was now standing. Our eyes met, and I couldn't look away as a jolt of electricity went through me.

It was as though nothing had changed over the years. She was just as beautiful as ever, if not more so, and I wanted her just as much. *Well, fuck.*

# CHAPTER 7

## EMILY

At first, I could barely believe my eyes. There was no way that it could possibly be Patrick Manning, my high school sweetheart, standing in front of me at the bar. *Shit, what the hell is he doing here?* I thought.

He looked even better than he had before, and I felt a twinge of remorse for throwing away what we had. He'd put on more muscle, and his jaw was more chiseled. Those piercing blue eyes were just the same as always though, and I couldn't look away from them.

"Hi, Emily," he greeted me, his voice smooth and soft. Lust shot right to my core at the sound of it. Just like it always had. I couldn't let him know how much he got to me, though. I wasn't sticking around in Saratoga, and things were different now. We could never go back to what we had had before, or anything like it.

I pasted on a smile. "Hey, Patrick," I said, as though it was no big deal to see him.

He wasn't wearing a suit or anything like that. Just dark-wash jeans and a flannel shirt. But success practically oozed from him. There was a confidence there. If I hadn't already known that he had done well for himself, I would have realized it then.

What were the chances that he would be back in Saratoga at the same time as me? I couldn't believe it.

Just one more kick from the universe, I supposed. Mocking me for the things that I had said to him on that last night. Our graduation night. I had been so full of myself back then. I had told him that there was no way that we could ever work out. That we were from different worlds. I had money, and he didn't.

Now I was being served up a cold dish of humble pie. He was the billionaire, and my family had next to nothing. How the tables had turned.

"What are you doing back here?" Alyssa asked him, and I was glad that she was the one to ask, because I wasn't sure that I could form words at the moment.

Patrick finally broke eye contact with me, turning toward her and grinning wryly. "If you can believe it, I'm here for an interview and a magazine shoot," he said.

"Wow, well aren't you fancy?" Alyssa asked.

"Uh, not really," Patrick said, looking uncomfortable for the first time. "It's just for some financial magazine, and they want to do, like, a rags-to-riches story about how I worked my way into the business world. They thought it would be a good idea to come back here to where it all began."

"Oh, wow," Alyssa said, her eyes widening. She giggled. "I mean, we all knew that you'd hit the big time, but a magazine shoot? That's amazing."

I barely heard what they were talking about. I couldn't seem to tear my eyes from Patrick. He had greeted me, but other than that, he had pretty much just dismissed me. He must remember my final words to him as well as I did. But where I had dismissed him before, it was his turn to remind me that I wasn't worthy of his attention now.

I waited for him to mention something about it. Now would be the perfect time for him to embarrass me in front of everyone, to have his revenge. All he had to do was say something casual about how he was richer than my family had ever been, after I had once dumped him because he wouldn't fit into my upper-class lifestyle.

I'd been such an asshole back then. It hadn't been all about the money. There had been other factors as well. And the scary thing was, when I really thought about it, I wasn't all that much different now.

I deserved every second of whatever shame he chose to heap on me. But of course, that wasn't Patrick. Instead, he made friendly conversation with Alyssa and Elliot. He glanced over at me occasionally, but I couldn't help feeling like he was pointedly ignoring me.

I felt tears stab the corners of my eyes. As though things weren't difficult enough at the moment, I now had to deal with this too. The worst part was, it didn't feel like I had any right to feel sorry for myself. After I had treated him so terribly, it was what I deserved. But I had to admit, his cool attitude toward me hurt all the same.

I quietly finished my drink, then leaned in to tell Alyssa that I was going to get a cab home. I couldn't sit there any longer. Alyssa nodded, but she barely seemed to have even heard me. I lingered for another moment, wondering if Patrick would say anything, but he was chatting with Elliot. Finally, I headed to the door alone.

I took in a deep breath when I made it outside, but the cool air did nothing to numb the ache in my chest. I pulled out my phone and opened the rideshare app, but before I could order a lift, Patrick appeared behind me.

"I'd be happy to give you a ride home," he said.

I blinked up at him, mouth open. I didn't even think he would realize that I had left. And now he was offering me a ride home? Before I could say anything, Patrick had linked his arm into mine and was leading me away down the street.

"We should get a move on before Alyssa realizes I've actually come after you rather than going to the bathroom like I told her," he said. "Last thing I need is to listen to her annoying laugh again."

I giggled, unable to help it. Then I covered my mouth with my hand, smacking his arm. "Alyssa's my friend," I reminded him.

Patrick shook his head, looking pained. "How do you cope with the laugh?" he asked. "Do you have hearing problems I wasn't aware of?"

I snorted again. This time, I didn't chastise him. I knew that I should probably pull away. What the hell was going on anyway? His touch was searing my arm even through my jacket, the heat suffusing my whole body.

By all rights, he should still be ignoring me. Maybe he was just using me as a convenient excuse to get away from Alyssa? It seemed almost like he actually wanted to be there, though. Like things were just the way that they had always been between us: comfortable and easy.

I swallowed hard, feeling tears prick the corners of my eyes again. I could let myself believe whatever the hell I wanted, but it wouldn't change things. There was no going back to how things were. Patrick was just taking me home, that was all. He had always been a nice guy. All he was doing was reminding me of that fact.

So that I would realize exactly what I had lost, all over again. That hurt more than any other revenge he could have concocted.

# CHAPTER 8

## PATRICK

I took a deep breath before I opened my car door. Emily had already gotten into the passenger's seat, and I just needed a moment to collect myself. Or maybe to pinch myself. Was this really happening? Emily Andrews was sitting in my car.

I hadn't expected to see her, let alone to get to talk to her. Not that we had really talked. She had barely said two words to me at the bar. I had initially thought that it was just because we were around everyone else, but now that we were on our own, she was still acting just as reserved. It bothered me, but I tried to ignore it.

She probably thought that I was still beneath her station, despite my abundance of money. A lot of people who'd been born into money saw "new money" as a dirty word. Oh well, it still spent the same. Still, if we were both going to be in town at the same time, there was no reason that we had to ignore and avoid one another, right? Saratoga Springs was only so big.

I slid into the car and started the engine. As we drove back toward her parents' mansion, I drummed my fingers against the steering wheel, trying to think of something to say. Finally, I just decided to ask her what was up. "Something wrong?" I asked.

Emily jumped and looked guiltily over at me. "No," she said.

"You're not happy to see me," I said, frowning out the windshield.

Emily sighed and looked out her window. "It's not that," she said. "I didn't expect to see you, that's all. I'm not unhappy to see you."

There were a lot of things that I wanted to say to her. I wanted to point out how wrong she had been about my potential. We might have been from two different worlds, but I had levelled the playing field. Hadn't I?

In the end, it wouldn't have been worth it. I could talk until I was blue in the face, but nothing she said would ever unbreak my heart.

She'd told me that she was in love with me once, but she hadn't even bothered to tell me that she was planning that gap year until it was already too late. Over the years, I'd realized that maybe she had never really cared for me at all. I'd been a nice piece of arm candy to escort her to school dances. The sex had been good. We had fun, but it was nothing more than that, and it was never meant to be.

Rehashing that now wouldn't solve anything. It would only end with me getting hurt all over again.

Suddenly, though, Emily turned away from the window and looked at me, really looked at me, like she was drinking in the sight of me, like she never wanted to forget it. The same way that I had when I saw her through the window at the bar.

I had been wrong. I knew that then. She truly had cared for me, once upon a time. She might still care for me. That didn't change the fact that things hadn't worked out between us, for whatever reason. But it wasn't that she had never had feelings for me. Things had never been that simple.

We pulled up in front of her parents' place. I was shocked to see the 'For Sale' sign in front of it. "For sale?" I asked Emily.

"You looking to buy?" she asked flippantly.

I blinked, surprised by her nonchalance. "Emily," I started to say, not even sure how to respond.

"Everything changes," she interrupted, before I could say anything else. She hopped out of the car. "Thanks for the ride." She shut the door, giving me one more long look before she walked off across the lawn to the house.

There was a part of me that wanted to get out and chase after her. She was upset; that much was obvious. I had thought initially that she was unhappy to see me there, but now I was sure that it was something bigger than that. The 'For Sale' sign was definitely a clue of some kind. But why were her parents selling the place? And why was Emily back here anyway?

A thousand terrible scenarios flashed through my imagination. I started the engine and headed back to the hotel. Once there, I couldn't help but open up my laptop. An easy internet search turned up about a dozen articles about the Andrews family. I read through a couple of them, feeling sick to my stomach.

The Andrews' were one of a dozen victims who lost everything to some Ponzi scheme. I could barely believe what I was reading. The house must be for sale because they couldn't afford to stay there. And Emily must be back in town because she couldn't afford to be anywhere else.

It only added to the irony of our breakup. She had

broken up with me once because we were from different worlds and it could never work out. I didn't have enough money to be part of her future. Now, I was the one on top, and her family had almost nothing left to their name. No wonder she had felt so awkward tonight.

I wondered who else knew. But of course, the whole town probably did. The only reason I didn't know was because I had carefully avoided any news about Saratoga Springs since I had left, knowing that it would bring me no happiness.

I shut my computer, staring blankly into the space where the articles had been. Again, I wanted to rush after her and comfort her. But we had closed the door on our relationship a long time ago.

# CHAPTER 9

## EMILY

Mom and I worked mostly in silence on Saturday afternoon as we packed up the kitchen. Dad was somewhere in his office, hopefully packing. I wrapped up the last of the glasses and set them carefully in the box, then turned to the next cabinet. Mom sniffled and dabbed at her eyes for the billionth time.

To be honest, I was doing most of the work on my own, and I had half a mind to tell her to go do something else. But I didn't really think she should be left to her own devices at the moment. Besides, she wasn't actively hindering the process of packing; she just wasn't being particularly productive.

I hadn't signed up to pack the whole house on my own, and I was starting to realize that I was going to be stuck in Saratoga for longer than I'd initially thought. We had a deadline, though; the movers were coming. I was just going to have to work faster, and maybe recruit some friends to help out.

The phone rang, startling both of us. I was honestly surprised to see that my parents still had a legitimate house phone in this day and age. I glanced over at Mom, but she didn't move to answer it. Finally, I grabbed it. "Hello?"

"Hey. Emily?"

I blinked in surprise. "Patrick?" I asked.

"Yeah," he said, sounding relieved to hear that it was me. "Listen, I'm in a bit of a bind, and I could use your help."

"Huh?" I asked, my mind racing. I couldn't for the life of me think of anything that I could help him out with. What was he up to?

"I'm doing this photo shoot for the magazine, but there's been a, um, wardrobe malfunction," Patrick said, sounding sheepish. "We need someone to help with the ensemble that I'm supposed to be wearing, but if we have to send all the way back to NYC for a new wardrobe person, we're going to lose the light. I really don't want to be stuck in Saratoga for any longer than I have to be."

"I know that feeling," I said wryly.

"I know you've always been great at fashion, and you're a whiz at sewing by hand. Can you come help?" Patrick asked hopefully. "We'll of course pay you. I know it's a last-minute thing, and I'll pay a premium even."

I was silent for a long moment. I considered refusing. But I could tell that his request was genuine. He wasn't trying to mock me and my newfound position; he really needed someone like me. And I could probably use the money. On the other hand, last night had proved how awkward things were between us now.

I glanced over at Mom. It would give me an excuse to get out of there for at least a little while, though. "All right," I said. "Here, let me give you my cellphone number. Text me where you need me. I'll be there as fast as I can."

"You're a lifesaver," Patrick said gratefully.

I gave him my number and then hung up. "I've got to go do something for a friend," I told Mom. "Can I borrow the car? I'll be back in a little while."

Mom sighed, and I could tell that it was on the tip of her tongue to remind me how much work we had left to do. But then, she seemed to remember how much I had done in comparison to her so far today. She nodded. "Keys are on the table by the door," she said.

I practically flew out of there, only pausing to grab my old sewing kit from my bedroom. I was surprised to see the address that Patrick sent me as I was getting into the car. The racetrack? I snorted and shook my head. All right, then.

When I got there, a staff member led me to a back room that held a disgruntled and half-dressed Patrick, an attractive man in a business suit, and a few other people who were probably from the magazine.

"You made it," Patrick said, relief on his face. He turned to the dude in the suit. "Jonah, this is Emily, the miracle-worker that I promised you. Emily, this is my business partner, Jonah."

"Nice to meet you," I said, dragging my eyes away from Patrick's bare chest.

How many times had I run my fingers along that chest? He was a little hairier now, and far more toned. But if I closed my eyes, I was sure I would have been able to feel the lingering memory of his warm, smooth skin beneath my cheek.

I shook those thoughts away. *Concentrate.*

"So as you can see, they want me dressed up as a jockey, but this stuff doesn't fit," Patrick said, rolling his eyes. "I tried to tell them that dressing up a hockey player as a jockey was probably a stupid idea, but they didn't listen."

"The *metaphor*," one of the magazine guys said, sounding disgusted by Patrick's attitude.

"Yeah, yeah," Patrick muttered. His business partner shot him a look, and he subsided into silence.

"Unfortunately, our wardrobe person is suffering from a nasty case of the stomach flu at the moment and can't leave her hotel room," Jonah explained to me. "Which means that we need someone to shoehorn Patrick into the clothes and make him look like something other than, well—"

"A jockey on steroids?" Patrick suggested wryly.

I couldn't bother hiding my amusement as I looked him over. It was a wonder those pants didn't split at the seams. As it was, I could see every detail of his body, including his tightly wrapped package. I blushed and snapped my gaze back up to his own. I grabbed the measuring tape out of my sewing kit, as well as a few other things.

"I can do this," I assured everyone. It was as though the whole room breathed a collective sigh of relief.

"Perfect," Jonah said. "You don't need me for this part, and since I have no interest in seeing Patrick's 'little jockey,' I'm going to go make some phone calls." He slipped out of the room.

"We're going to go finish setting up the rest of the shoot," the photographer said, gesturing toward his companions. "Please work quickly. The weather is supposed to be terrible tomorrow, so if we lose the light, I'm afraid it could be a few days before we can try again."

Patrick looked pained at the thought of that, and I grinned. "I'll see what I can do," I promised the photographer.

Then it was just Patrick and me alone in the room. I jotted down some measurements, trying to focus on my task.

It was hard to do, though, as I ran the tape along his body, my fingers trailing along his bare skin. I was close enough, of course, that I could smell his distinctly masculine scent. Was that the same spicy cologne that he used to wear in school, or was I imagining it?

"Sorry about this," he said as I worked. "Like I said, I knew it was a dumb idea from the start, but everyone seemed to think it was perfect."

"Don't worry about it," I said to him, staring down at the material in front of me and thinking about what I could do. A couple of inserts here and there and I was sure we could patch something together that would fit him. If I could just keep from getting distracted.

I glanced up at him and then looked quickly back down. Big mistake. He was still my half-naked, chiseled god of an ex-boyfriend. I swallowed hard.

"Actually, this is good practice for me," I told him as I started ripping out a seam in the jacket. "I'm actually working on a degree in fashion design. Although I'm more used to working on dummies than on people."

"You know, Jonah would probably still say that you were working on a dummy," Patrick joked, and I laughed in spite of myself.

"Here, can you get changed back into your other clothes for a bit?" I asked him. "I need to work on those pants. I have a feeling if you move at all, it's only a matter of time before you split the seams." It also had the added benefit of getting him back into clothes that would hopefully cover him up some. Otherwise, I was never going to get anything done before the photographer lost the light.

"Split the seams, or castrate myself," Patrick muttered. He turned his back as he changed, but he was still right there in the room with me. I tried not to look, but I couldn't help peeking over a couple times. My mouth went dry as I caught a glimpse of his naked body. My cheeks flushed, and I could feel my core tighten with heat and desire.

I hurriedly focused on threading the needle that was in my hands, trying to get my mind off of him. I had given him up a long time ago now. Why was it still so hard to be alone in the room with him?

I pushed those thoughts away. *Just concentrate on the task.* That was all I could do. The last thing I wanted was to make things even more awkward between us.

# CHAPTER 10

## PATRICK

I had to admit; I was impressed with the quick work that Emily did to modify the jockey costume. I almost didn't call her, actually. When I first couldn't fit into the outfit, I had taken it as a sign that the whole thing was ludicrous. The photographer was talking about how he just had to have this shot and how we were going to be stuck there for days if we 'lost the light' now. But I could have vetoed that and told him to take the shoot in another direction.

After all, it wasn't my fault that they hadn't gotten an outfit that fit me. It wasn't exactly a secret that I was a fair bit larger than your average jockey, even if the costume was an XL. What did I care if they didn't get the shot that they wanted? So what if we lost the light?

Then I thought about Emily. I remembered how skilled she was at sewing and fashion, and I recognized the opportunity there. I could spend the day with her, a day while she was occupied by her craft and not by the awkwardness of our former relationship.

I was under no illusions; as much as I might have wished for the chance to hold her one more time, I knew that it wasn't to be. Still, maybe it would help distract her from her family's plight.

So far, it seemed to be working. She pieced together the outfit as I sat and scrolled through my phone, peeking over at her every so often to watch her work. I didn't want to make her feel too nervous or like I was staring her down, but I couldn't help wanting to watch her. She was adorable like that, her brow wrinkled with concentration and her tongue just poking out between her teeth. I could barely see the tiny stitches that she put into the material.

Finally, she lifted her head with a smile. "All right, let's try this," she said, shaking out the modified costume. "You'll have to let me help you into it. Hand-sewing this quickly isn't quite as durable as machine-sewing, and I'd hate to have you rip out all the work I just did. I think that photographer would kill us."

I laughed. "Probably," I agreed. I stripped off my shirt first, and she helped me into the jockey's top. Where before, I had barely been able to get my arms into the thing, this time it fit like a glove. I couldn't think about that, though. Couldn't think about anything to do with Emily and the jockey costume. Because if I thought about it too hard, I was going to start thinking about Emily's competent hands on my body, smoothing across the fabric. The last thing I needed right now was an erection.

I focused on my breathing, filling my head with thoughts about how ridiculous I probably looked. I was sure I would get tons of chirps from my former teammates when the spread came out. Somehow, though, that only led me to thinking of the rink where I had first asked Emily out. Unlike the women who threw themselves at me now, Emily had made me chase her. And I liked that.

Finally, Emily was done piecing together the costume.

She took a step back, nodding approvingly. "Not my best work, but I think it'll do," she said, eyeing the outfit critically.

I turned to look at myself in the mirror, surprised to see what she had done. She had managed to keep the integrity of the uniform while adding in some extra material that she had procured from somewhere. I frowned, squinting at the red fabric that she had sewn into spots where the costume was too tight. "Is this from your prom dress?" I asked her in shock.

She blushed and looked off to the side. "It was what I had in my kit for scraps," she said. "Must have been the last project that I worked on before I got that new kit for graduation."

We were both quiet for a moment. I wondered if she was thinking back to prom as well. We had gone together, of course. I had never seen her look more beautiful than the moment that she walked down the stairs at her parents' mansion, when I had come to pick her up. I had known that she was making her own dress for the occasion, but I never could have imagined how professional and incredible that dress had looked. I wondered if she still had it.

The photographer came in, interrupting the moment. "Perfect, you're dressed," he said to me. He eyed the outfit just as critically as Emily had. "I don't love the addition of red into the outfit, but it'll work." He caught my arm and practically dragged me out to the racetrack.

I expected Emily to leave then. After all, she had done what we needed her to do, and I doubted she wanted to stick around for the whole photo shoot. But to my surprise, she followed us out to the track.

"All right, we've got this whole track rented for the day and it's costing the magazine a pretty penny, so let's get going," Jonah said, nodding approvingly at me. He glanced over at Emily. "You did good work."

"Thanks," she said, blushing and ducking her head. She hopped up on one of the railings and took a seat. Matt got things rolling with the shoot.

"No, not like that," he said about half an hour later, sounding exasperated. "Would you just loosen up? Relax a little."

I grimaced and tried my best to relax. I had never been very comfortable in front of a camera. And why the hell did it have to be here? If I were doing something more natural for these shots, I was sure I would have felt a lot more comfortable.

Emily distracted me as she moved behind Matt and his assistant. I tried to focus on the camera, but she started waving her arms around. I looked back at her and tried not to laugh as I saw the face she was making at me.

"Oh, that's great!" Matt said, sounding relieved, and I suddenly realized what Emily was actually doing. She wasn't just bored and making fun of the shoot. She was trying to make me laugh, to get me to relax.

She kept pulling faces, and I could practically feel the tension dropping away from me. After that, it was quick work for Matt to get what he wanted. "These are going to be perfect," he said enthusiastically as we packed everything up.

"Great," I said, feeling relieved. One photo shoot down. As my eyes slid over to Emily, I realized that I wasn't dying to get out of Saratoga Springs anymore.

She followed me back to my dressing room. "I'm not sure I can get out of this on my own," I confessed, laughing a little.

Emily grinned. "Probably not, or at least without tearing the length of the thing," she agreed. "I'll help you."

Back in the dressing room, she helped me out of my clothes. We were standing so close to one another, and I couldn't help thinking of the other times when she had stripped me down naked. I wanted to kiss her, but I held myself in check. She wouldn't appreciate that.

I couldn't help getting aroused as I finally stood in front of her in just my underwear. I swallowed hard and turned my back, feeling embarrassed as I grabbed my normal clothes.

"I'll, uh, wait outside," Emily said, and I mentally cursed my half-hard cock. I couldn't help feeling attracted to her or thinking about our earlier relationship. But now I'd gone and scared her off. She would probably head back home now without even saying goodbye, sure that the only reason I had called her at all was because I was hoping to, I don't know, have sex with her in the dressing room or whatever.

It wasn't like that. Even if she had indicated that she was still interested in me, I would have wanted to do things right. I would have wanted to take her out to dinner, do something romantic.

It was Emily, after all. My high school sweetheart. She didn't deserve to be treated as though she was just a fling.

*Even if that's how she'd treated me.*

I shook my head and finished getting dressed. I was surprised to see that Emily was still hanging around, chatting with Jonah near the snack counter. "That's much more you," she teased, eyeing my jeans and flannel.

I laughed. "Yeah, definitely." I shrugged. "It's nice to be back in something that fits right, too." I paused. "Thanks again for helping out today. You were a lifesaver." I fished out my wallet and pulled out the blank check that I always carried in case of unexpected business expenses. I quickly filled it out and handed it over to her.

Emily's eyes got wide. "Patrick, this is way too much," she said. She bit her lower lip. "You know, you don't have to pay me more because of...my situation."

Oh Christ, she thought I was only paying her that much because I felt sorry about her family's loss of fortune. I could have kicked myself. "It has nothing to do with that," I said, shaking my head. "You really helped me out today. And I told you I would pay you extra for the short notice. Besides, this magazine spread is a publicity thing. So my business is going to benefit, all because you had a way of making things work for the shoot."

"I guess so," Emily said, still looking unconvinced.

"You should have paid her double for having to work in close proximity to your naked body," Jonah piped in, his eyes twinkling.

Finally, Emily laughed and folded the check to put in her pocket. "Thanks," she said. She paused. "I guess I'll see you around?"

"Yeah, I should be around for a little while longer, at least," I said. To be honest, I didn't want her to go already, but I was afraid that if I asked her to join me for dinner, even if Jonah tagged along, it would make her uncomfortable.

Emily nodded and gave me a little wave. With that, she was gone.

And already, I found myself missing her.

## CHAPTER 11

### EMILY

I worked for half the night on Saturday trying to pack up things around the house. I wanted to ask Mom if she had bothered to do anything at all while I was gone, but I knew that it was a difficult time for her. If she hadn't done anything, it was only because she was too upset at losing her whole life.

I managed to get a couple rooms boxed up over the course of the night. It helped that I couldn't sleep. I felt wired in a weird way. Restless. My mind kept going back around to the feeling of my fingers brushing across Patrick's skin.

I was turned on, I had to admit. I wasn't going to do anything about it – no reason to train my brain into thinking that it was all right for me to want Patrick that way. That ship had sailed nearly a decade ago now. I was worried that if I tried to go to bed and just sleep it off, I would end up dreaming about him. I wasn't sure which was worse.

I felt silly for being this affected by him, to be honest. I mean, he was sexy as all get-out, but it wasn't like I hadn't dated anyone else since I had been with him. I was over

Patrick. There was a reason that things hadn't worked out between us.

I was quickly forgetting what those reasons were, though. Surely it hadn't been all about money, or about the fact that I was scared that I was falling too in love with him at too young an age. There were other reasons as well but at the moment I couldn't come up with a single one. Every time I went down that line of thought, I just couldn't figure out why I had broken up with him.

Even still, I shouldn't have been so wrapped up in the idea of him now. He was sexy, he was smart, and there was a history there. He was the guy who'd taken my virginity. But we were both way different people now. Things wouldn't work out. Besides, I wasn't planning on staying around in Saratoga Springs for any longer than was necessary, and it didn't sound like Patrick planned to stick around either.

Despite the fact that I went to bed well after midnight, I found myself wide awake early on Sunday morning. The first thing I did was run to the shop to get more tape and a marker. Then I settled in to taping up and labeling the boxes that I had packed the night before.

I was practically buried by boxes when I heard the doorbell ring. I had a feeling that neither of my parents would feel much like answering it. I didn't want to be interrupted, but maybe it was something important.

I did my best to disentangle myself from the mess that I had created, hurdling over one of the boxes on my way to the front door. I skidded across the tiles in my socked feet and breathlessly pulled open the door.

I felt myself blushing as I stared at Patrick standing there on my doorstep. Suddenly, snatches of a dream from the previous night came flowing unbidden into my mind. He had been naked, there in the shower with me. He had traced my skin with his tongue, his fingers working into the slick opening at the apex of my thighs. I could practically feel the cool tiles beneath my fingertips as Patrick raised an eyebrow at me. I fought not to shudder with the memory.

"Hey, you all right?" he asked.

"Uh, yeah," I said, stepping back to let him in. "I'm just trying to get some things packed up for my parents and there was a bit of mess between the door and me."

Patrick laughed. "Fair enough," he said. "Are they staying in Saratoga Springs?"

"Yeah, but they're downsizing to a condo," I said. It was the answer that I'd been telling everyone. Close enough to the truth without getting into it too much.

My parents couldn't afford this place anymore. Not after my dad lost it all.

Patrick looked around the hall with interest, and I was suddenly reminded of the fact that he had never been there before. Back when we were dating, I'd been careful to keep things a secret from my parents. I knew that they would never approve of him. They wanted me to end up with someone rich, the kind of guy who was going to go places and could keep me in the lifestyle to which I'd become accustomed.

I had never even introduced Patrick to them, not even as a friend. I had never even given him a chance. Jesus, what a stuck-up bitch I'd been.

Guilt came flooding back to me all over again. God, I'd been so terrible to him. It was a wonder that he'd put up with me for as long as he had. I distinctly remembered him planning our future together. He wanted us to live together in the dorms for our freshman year. He wanted us to get a place together after.

I had blown him off like I had never even considered that we might have a future. Maybe I hadn't.

In the present, Patrick turned back to me, a crooked grin on his face. "Anyway, I just wanted to tell you again how much I appreciated you saving my bacon yesterday. I mean, I know I already thanked you, but seriously, you're a lifesaver."

I shrugged uncomfortably. "It was nothing," I said. He had paid me way more than he should have for the work that I had done, but I had been so stupidly grateful for that money that I had barely protested.

"Actually, I've got an offer for you, if you're interested," Patrick continued.

"What sort of offer?" I asked, immediately suspicious.

"I don't know how much you know about my company, but basically, we're an outdoor retail startup. We're looking to launch our own line of outdoor clothing, but I've been having some problems with the team. Specifically, I'm having a difficult time communicating what I want and getting prototypes put together for the designs."

"Okay," I said slowly. "So you were hoping I'd help you sketch out some of what you're thinking?"

"It's a bit more than that," Patrick said, rubbing the back of his neck. "I can be, ah, a little difficult to work with sometimes. I'm very particular about what I want because if it's got my name on it, it has to be perfect. Anyway, my head designer quit last week, and I have yet to hire anyone new. I was wondering if you'd be interested in the position?"

I frowned at him. "I haven't finished my degree yet," I told him slowly. "Besides, I don't know anything about the outdoor industry. You know I'm not exactly the sportiest person out there."

"That's honestly kind of a good thing," Patrick said,

shrugging. "We're hoping to appeal to a broader audience than just the 'sportiest people out there.' Plus, I have a good idea of what I want. Like I said, I'm just having a hard time communicating it. You know that's never been my strongest suit. I'm a hockey player." He grinned crookedly at me. "And regarding your degree, I won't tell if you don't."

I could barely believe what I was hearing. "Why are you doing this?" I finally asked. "I know we didn't split on the best of terms. So why would you make me this offer now?"

Patrick smiled at me, giving a little shrug. "You did an amazing job yesterday," he said. "And look, I know why your parents are selling the house and all of that. I know that you probably think I'm just doing this out of pity or as some cruel joke. But I really do want to make sure that you're all right. I do want to help you, if I can."

I sighed and looked unhappily away from him. "Patrick, you can't just give me a job like this because you feel sorry for me," I told him.

"I'm not" Patrick countered. "Well, not completely," he admitted when I shot him a look. "I wouldn't have offered you the job if I didn't think that you could handle it." He paused. "It's a huge opportunity, Emily. I know that the fashion world is all about who you know and the connections that you make. The business world works the same way. You and I are both lucky to have this connection. I think you could be just what my company needs."

I wanted to protest more, but I had always trusted Patrick. If he thought that I was what he needed for his company, then that was the truth.

But could I handle working alongside him? Trying to untangle his thoughts and put them together into some semblance of coherence that the other people on the project could work off of?

"Where do you even live at this point?" I suddenly blurted out. Oddly enough, that hadn't been in any of the gossip that Alyssa had told me about town.

Was I going to have to move to wherever Patrick was living at the moment? The thought made a small shiver of anticipation run along my spine. Just Patrick and me, in some distant city. What would happen to us away from Saratoga Springs? It would be as though the slate had been wiped clean. We would get a second chance.

Did Patrick want a second chance as badly as I suddenly did?

Patrick laughed. "I'm living in Boston at the moment," he said. "I thought you knew that. Moved there to play hockey and never left." He shrugged. "But we've got an office here too that I'm working out of at the moment. For this position, I'd need you in the office here to start with, but once you've got a handle on the company and everything, it's set up to be location independent. You can keep your apartment in New York, and if you're still in school, you'll have the flexibility to schedule things as needed around your classes. All I ask is that you conference call with the other designers and me a few times a week so that we can make sure that we're all on the same page."

"Oh," I said, frowning. I didn't want to ask how much he'd be paying me, but I had a feeling that it would be more than the minimum wage jobs that I'd been looking at. Besides, even if I needed to put college on hold for the time being, it would mean that I could keep my apartment and get a little more real-world experience in the industry that would make my résumé look stellar when I actually applied for a long-term career.

I nodded slowly. "All right," I said. "I'll do it."

Patrick's grin was brighter than the sun. "Excellent," he said, reaching out to shake hands with me.

Sparks flew as I held his callused hand in mine. I looked up at him in surprise, my eyes widening. Was he feeling this same thing? A memory of the way that we had been together, tinged with the promise of a different sort of future.

Maybe we would never go back to the way we had once been. Maybe we would only work together, nothing more than that. But maybe that wasn't such a bad future after all. If nothing else, it would be good to have my friend Patrick back in my life again.

Whatever Patrick was thinking, it didn't show in his expression. Reluctantly, I let go of his hand.

Maybe there was some small sliver of hope for us after all.

Patrick dug his wallet out of his pocket and fished in it for a business card, which he handed over to me. "That's the address for the Saratoga office," he said. "I'll expect to see you there tomorrow morning." With that, he left.

I stared down at the card in my hand, absently tracing the embossed letters of his name.

*Patrick Manning.*

I just hoped I wasn't making a huge mistake.

# CHAPTER 12

## PATRICK

Come Monday morning, I was more nervous than I would have expected. I knew that I had done the right thing in hiring Emily. Like I had told her, it was partly about the fact that I knew what her family was going through at the moment. I wanted to help her. I could only imagine how things were for her right now.

But it was more than that. I really did believe that she was the person for the job. I had seen the work that she did on Saturday at the racetrack. She was a whiz. I didn't care if she wasn't done with her degree or not; she had clearly demonstrated that she knew what she was doing when it came to design. I needed someone like that on my team.

I hadn't been lying when I told her that I was difficult to work with. That was the general consensus on the team. It was just frustrating to me, because I knew what I wanted, in my head, but I didn't know how to communicate it properly. I didn't have any sort of experience in the design realm, and it showed.

I needed someone like Emily who knew me well enough that she could figure out what I was thinking.

what I wanted. She had always been able to do that before, and I had a feeling it wasn't going to be any different now. It was nothing that she wouldn't be able to handle.

At the same time, I was nervous that we were going to be working closely together. It had been difficult enough to keep my hands off of her the other day at the track, and that was just one afternoon. What would happen when we were working together regularly?

But no, I told myself. The only reason the other day had been particularly difficult was because Emily had literally had her hands all over my body. The new arrangement would be a lot more professional.

Jonah raised an eyebrow at me, noting my fidgeting. "What's up with you today?" he asked. "Everything all right?"

I grinned wryly. Of course he would notice my agitation. I wasn't exactly making a secret of it. "You remember Emily?"

"Of course," Jonah said, frowning at me. "What, did you guys hook up or something?"

"Nothing like that," I said, shaking my head. "But I did hire her to be the new head designer for our clothing line." It wasn't like I could keep that a secret from him, after all. I held my breath as I waited for my business partner's response. I probably should have run the idea by him before I hired Emily. I supposed it technically wasn't too late for him to protest since Emily hadn't signed any of the paperwork yet or anything.

There was no way I could handle revoking the offer, though. I couldn't risk disappointing Emily, pulling the rug out from under her at the worst time in her life.

Jonah shook his head. "What's the deal with you and

that hometown beauty anyway?" he asked bluntly. "What are her qualifications for this job? It's a big deal, you know."

"I know," I said, trying not to sound too peeved at the question. I knew that if our positions were reversed, I would have been a little suspicious as well. "She's talented. You saw that the other day. And she's good under pressure."

"Sure, I saw her piece together a costume for you. That's a lot different than designing a whole line of outdoor apparel," Jonah said, sounding pained.

"I get that, but I'm telling you she can do it," I said. "You know that I mostly just need her to be able to help me get my thoughts down on paper. And she's gone to school for fashion and design, plus had a bunch of internships at big design houses. She's good."

"Okay," Jonah said, but he still sounded somewhat doubtful. "Just, I'm not stupid. I can tell that there's some, shall we say, unfinished business between the two of you."

I shook my head. "It's all history," I promised him. "We dated back in high school, but we haven't seen one another or talked in years now. I promise I wouldn't have brought her on if I didn't think she had talent. You know how much this business means to me."

I didn't want to tell him about her family's current financial problems and the fact that Emily probably really needed the job. It was just about her talent, I told myself. That was the reason I wanted her on the project, not because I had a desperate need to help her out.

Jonah sighed. "I know, this company is your baby. I just hope she's all that you've said she is and more, because we really can't afford any more setbacks."

My assistant, Faith, knocked on the door to my office and poked her head in. "Patrick? There's a woman here to see you. Emily Andrews? There's no appointment in your calendar, but she says that you hired her as a designer?"

"Yes, I did," I said, smiling warmly at the woman. "Go ahead and send her in, please."

Faith nodded and disappeared. A couple moments later, she was replaced by Emily. "Hey, Jonah. Patrick." She nodded at the two of us, smiling warmly. "I hope I'm not too late. I was trying to help Mom with a little more packing this morning before I came over."

"This is perfect," I assured her, the words barely one step away from a croak. I couldn't help it. She looked amazing. I had never seen her in professional dress before, but she made it look *good*. Her hair was pulled into a high bun, and she was wearing a black polka-dot blouse with a lipstick-red pencil skirt. Pair that with some black heels and her curves were on full display. I absently took a sip of my coffee; my mouth having gone dry.

From the corner of my eye, I could see Jonah roll his eyes in exasperation, but at that moment, I didn't give a damn. He was a dude; even if he didn't have a history with her, he had eyes. He must be able to see how drop-dead sexy she looked right then.

"Welcome to the team, Emily," Jonah said, getting to his feet. He looked over at me. "I've got to get to work. Matt said he'd send over some of the photos from the other day's shoot for you to okay, and then don't forget that Alex wanted to chat with you over lunch again."

"Right," I said, looking back at him. My eyes drifted back to Emily again within moments, though. I cleared my throat. "I guess I should bring you to HR so you can sign all your paperwork, and then I'll introduce you to the other designers."

"Sounds good," Emily said brightly. She followed me

through the office to HR. I waited outside, checking emails on my phone as they got her all set up. Then I led her down one floor to the design lab.

"Everyone, this is Emily," I announced. "She's going to be the new head designer on the project. She's an absolute genius with every part of the design process, and I expect you guys are going to love her. She'll be my new go-between with you guys, too, so you can stop trying to figure out what the heck I'm ranting about all the time."

There were laughs around the office.

I continued, "Sophie, do you think you can take a little time this morning to get her all caught up to speed on the project as it currently stands?"

"Sure thing, Boss," Sophie said, giving me a smart-ass salute that made me grin.

"Great. I'm going to show her to her office first, but then she's all yours," I said.

"Perfect," Sophie said. "I'm reading through the weekend's emails and things anyway, so if you can give me twenty minutes, half an hour, that'll be perfect."

I nodded at her and steered Emily toward her new office. "Here it is," I said, closing the door behind us.

Emily nodded, but I could see anxiety filling her eyes. I blinked in surprise. I hadn't even realized that she was nervous when she first came in. She hid it well. But now that it was just the two of us, behind closed doors, it was as though all of that pretense just slipped away.

Without thinking, I moved forward, folding her into my arms. "Take a deep breath," I murmured into her hair. I felt her do just that as her arms slowly crept around me. She leaned into me, taking obvious comfort from my solid warmth.

"You can do this," I told her firmly. "You have all the

training and the talent. All you needed was the opportunity. And here it is."

Emily finally pulled back, blinking up at me. "How do you know?" she asked. "I've only had one job before, working twenty hours a week as a retail clerk in a fashion boutique."

"Bullshit," I told her, shaking my head. "I did some research on you, Emily. I know all about those internships that you've had."

"They weren't paid," Emily said weakly.

"And? They're still valuable experience. Plus, I know you," I said, shrugging. "I bet for the amount that you threw yourself into your work there, they should have been paying you a king's ransom."

Emily sighed. "Still, how am I supposed to lead an entire team? I've never done anything like this before." She sounded stressed, and I knew there was already so much going on in her life that the added worry was the last thing she needed. Had I made a mistake in hiring her? Had I miscalculated?

But I was sure that she was perfect for the position. Impostor syndrome was normal. It didn't mean that she wouldn't be amazing. In fact, I would have been worried if she wasn't nervous, as it probably would have meant that she wasn't taking it seriously.

I cupped her face in my palms, unable to resist dragging the pad of my thumb across her cheekbone. She looked so vulnerable, and it made me want to make everything all better for her. I couldn't do that, but I could give her a little pep talk.

"I've never had more confidence in another person than I do in you right now," I told her quietly. "I know that you can do this."

Emily stared up at me for a long moment. Then a slow and tremulous smile spread across her face. That smile went right to my core, energizing me.

Instead of letting her go, like I knew I needed to do, I leaned in until our mouths were mere inches apart. "I've missed you," I whispered against her lips.

Then I kissed her.

# CHAPTER 13

## EMILY

I was mildly surprised when Patrick leaned in to kiss me, but it didn't take long for me to surrender to the sensation. My whole body felt electrified; I felt alive in a way that I hadn't in a long time now. It was such a silly thing, but I couldn't help remembering how well he and I fit together. It had always been as though our bodies already knew one another's. I had expected that my first real relationship would be awkward and clumsy, but it just never had been with Patrick.

I opened my mouth to him, letting him push his tongue against mine. Jolts of pleasure burst inside of me, and I couldn't help moaning. I knew that we probably shouldn't be doing this—not here, at work, on my first day, and especially not in light of our history—but I couldn't bring myself to pull away from him.

The kiss was even better than I remembered. For a moment, I lost myself in it, unable to think about how inappropriate it was.

But suddenly, it all came crashing back. I came to my senses and pulled away, staring up at him with wide eyes.

Patrick's eyes were dark with desire, and he looked for all the world like he wanted nothing more than to kiss me again.

Slowly, he blinked and then took a hasty step back, seeming to realize himself as well. He swore under his breath. "Sorry," he muttered. "I forgot myself."

He sounded sheepish. Embarrassed. I wanted to tell him not to apologize. It took two people to kiss. I definitely hadn't been pulling away from him, at least not at first.

Did I want things to progress between us again? I didn't think I wanted a relationship with him. There was too much history there, and I had enough chaos in my life at the moment. Besides, I wasn't planning on sticking around Saratoga Springs for any longer than I had to, and I definitely wasn't about to move to Boston to be with him. That would have been crazy.

*Would it?* I couldn't resist asking myself that question. Would it be so crazy for me to move to Boston to be with Patrick? He was my high school sweetheart, the first boy I'd ever loved. I'd never met anyone else who complemented me more perfectly.

I was getting ahead of myself, though. All we had done was kiss, and Patrick was acting as though that had been some colossal mistake.

"Seriously, I promise to behave like a professional from here on out," he was saying. "You don't have to worry."

"I wasn't worried," I said quietly, but I didn't know what else to say. Regret filled Patrick's face. Of course he wouldn't really want to get back together with me. I had stomped all over his heart once, telling him that he wasn't good enough for me.

Now he was the one who was my boss. He was the one with the money, with the whole world at his feet. I couldn't even get through a day of work without having a breakdown to my new boss about how I didn't think I had enough experience for the job.

I had to start acting professionally as well. Patrick was my boss now, and I had to treat him as my boss, not as anything more familiar.

I squared my shoulders and took in a deep breath. "We'll both be more professional," I promised Patrick. I looked around the office. "I guess I'd better get acquainted with the job."

"Right," Patrick said, sounding relieved at my understanding. "I'll get out of your hair and send Sophie in with the design book."

He disappeared before I could say anything else.

Fortunately, Sophie came in before I had too much time to dwell on what had just happened. "All right," she said, dropping a heavy book on my desk. "This is the design book. Let's take a look."

We pulled our seats close together, and I forced myself to pay close attention as she showed me the book and the pieces that they were working on. I had to smile at the copious notes on each page. I recognized that scrawling handwriting, although I hadn't seen it since the days of lab reports and Spanish homework.

Patrick.

It was clear from the notes that he had jotted down there that he had some very specific ideas, some of which were going to be a real challenge to make a reality. I asked Sophie several questions, only some of which she could answer. It was clear that Patrick and the rest of the design team weren't exactly on the same page. We'd need to fix that first.

I nodded, already making a mental list of questions that

I needed to ask. At least it would be easier to keep things between Patrick and me professional if we just focused on the task in front of us. And I had to admit, I was excited for the chance. I still felt a little bit out of my depth, but at the same time, I loved projects that would force me to think outside the box. They tended to be where I did my best work.

"Any prototypes yet?" I finally asked as we got through the book.

"Yeah," Sophie said. "Here, I'll show you. I'm warning you, though, they're definitely a little rough."

I nodded and followed her to the wardrobe room. I could immediately see what she meant about them being works in progress. I had my work cut out for me.

*First things first, make sure that everyone is on the same page*, I thought. For that, I needed to schedule some time to chat with Patrick more about his vision and the notes that he had written in the design book. Then I would be able to make a solid plan.

Surprisingly, as we moved through my first week working for Patrick, I started to feel more and more confident about my role there. The rest of the designers were great, and there were times when I was sure that one of them should have been the head designer instead. But overall, I felt as though it was the job that I had been training for my whole life. I was starting to feel comfortable coming up with the plan and asking people to do whatever I needed of them.

It was partly that Patrick kept things pretty relaxed around the office. But it was also about *me*.

I got to know the team that was working for me, making a mental list of their talents, already planning who would be perfect for each task on our list as we moved forward. I knew that we were on a tight timeline. Patrick wanted the line launched as soon as possible. There had already been a number of delays, including the loss of the former head designer due to "artistic differences" or some bullshit like that, according to Sophie.

I worked long hours, glad for the excuse to get out of my parents' house. I was still helping them pack up, as much as I could. We were getting there, but it was nice to be able to do most of the packing on my own, late at night. It was a relief not to have to deal with the dreary atmosphere—Mom's tears and Dad's listlessness.

I couldn't tell Patrick how much I appreciated the chance that he was giving me. Instead, I set out to show him just how much I deserved it. I hadn't seen much of him since that kiss, and I had to admit, I was a little disappointed in that, even though I knew it was for the best. I had too much other stuff to deal with right now, and anyway, he was my boss. I didn't need my reputation in the fashion world to be tarnished by a scandal like that.

In my darker moments, I wondered if the reason he'd been so hands-off was that he'd gotten it all out of his system and was no longer interested in me. I didn't like to think about that, though.

To be honest, I had enjoyed the kiss more than I had thought possible. I didn't want to return to how things were. There was too much between us for that. But was it possible for us to date again, this time as adults?

I supposed I would never know. Patrick was too focused on his company and its success for that. It was my fault that things had gotten messed up, so it wasn't like I could blame him.

When Patrick called me on Friday morning and asked me to meet with him that afternoon to go over our week's progress, though, I couldn't help but want to impress him. I agreed to the meeting, and then I immediately started to prep.

Maybe I could never have him back, but I was going to keep the job if it killed me. I was going to make Patrick see that he hadn't made a mistake in giving me an opportunity. That was the best that I could do, and it was just going to have to be good enough.

# CHAPTER 14

## PATRICK

I didn't want to say that I was avoiding Emily. Even if I was, there was a reason for it, and that reason was the kiss.

The kiss. I was trying hard not to think about the kiss.

Trouble was, every time I happened to see her, that was what popped into my head. The feeling of her body pressed against mine and my tongue twining with hers. I knew from her reaction that I'd been out of line, though. Hell, I didn't know, maybe she had a boyfriend back in New York City.

I shouldn't have kissed her. Especially not since I was her boss now. I knew that I was going to have to keep my hands to myself. Avoiding her made things a little easier on me.

Except I wasn't avoiding her, I reminded myself. It was just that we worked on different floors and there was no reason to interact any more than we had to. She had asked me a few questions about some of the notes in the design book, but other than that, she had stuck with the designers. I knew that she had been working hard. I was excited to see what she had to share with me on Friday.

I just hoped I could concentrate on the meeting and not on all the other things that I'd rather be doing with her there in my office. I actually thought about inviting Jonah to sit in on the meeting as well, but he had other things that he needed to do, and I couldn't drag him away. He was getting ready to head back to Boston soon since I would be staying in Saratoga longer than I'd anticipated to make sure things with Emily were running smoothly. I was sure that my need for supervision would only make things more awkward for all parties anyway.

I couldn't help it; I liked Emily. I had always liked Emily. She was even more beautiful now than she used to be, and she had grown a lot as a person. She no longer seemed so full of herself. She seemed a lot more self-aware and that was very attractive to me.

Almost too attractive. My assistant knocked on my door. "Emily just asked me to let you know that she's ready in the conference room for your meeting."

"Thanks, Faith," I told her.

I was surprised when Faith hovered in the doorway for a moment. "If you don't mind me asking, where did you meet this new chief designer?" she asked. She held up a hand. "I know it's not my place to question any of it. It's just that when I was putting in her HR paperwork in the system, I saw that she doesn't really have a ton of experience. She doesn't even have a degree."

"She's more than qualified," I said firmly. "She knows what she's doing." I paused and then added, "She's an old friend of mine, actually. We haven't seen one another in years, but we recently reconnected. That's not why I hired her, though. She helped me out with a wardrobe malfunction when I was doing that magazine spread last weekend. I realized that she was just what I was looking for here."

"Okay," Faith said, sounding unconvinced. "I just want to make sure you're being careful. What are the chances that an old friend just happens to come back into your life just when you're starting to really make a name for yourself in the business world?"

I laughed. "Faith, I appreciate the advice, but trust me on this one. Emily isn't a gold-digger."

Faith frowned and then stepped further into the office, shutting the door behind herself. "Look, I'm sure you know her better than I do. I did a little digging into her family, though, and it sounds like they're having pretty serious money troubles. Are you sure that she's not just interested in you because of your money?"

I sighed. "I know all about that," I promised Faith. "To be honest, it is part of the reason why I wanted to give Emily a chance. I know a little something about money troubles. I wanted to help her out, and I have the means to do so these days. But she's not interested in anything more than a job from me. She's not interested in dating me, or whatever else it is that you're implying."

Faith gave me a look like she didn't believe me, but she shrugged. "All right," she said. "It's obviously your call. Just be careful, all right?"

I smiled at her. I was always selective when it came to hiring new workers for the company. I didn't want the place to feel stuffy. Honestly, if you had told my younger self that I would one day end up working in an office, I think I would have died a little bit inside. I wanted the place to feel like the anti-office. I wanted friendly workers who were all passionate about the outdoors.

Somehow, I had managed to find friendly employees who were all loyal to each other too. The kind of co-workers who really cared about one another. Faith had been with

Jonah and me from the beginning and was just looking out for me; making sure that I wasn't being taken advantage of.

In all honesty, I was afraid that things would appear to be more the opposite; that I was taking advantage of Emily. After all, I was her boss. She was going through a bunch of stuff with her family, and she was vulnerable. I had seen that vulnerability there in her eyes, just before I'd kissed her. If anyone was being taken advantage of here, it was Emily.

Of course, I wasn't about to get into that with Faith.

"The first sign that she's incompetent or of any sort of impropriety, she's out," I promised my assistant as I got to my feet. "In any case, I should probably head to the conference room now so I can see her report from the week. Hopefully our outdoor apparel line is coming along smoothly."

"Finally," Faith said wryly. She smiled and returned to her desk. I headed for the conference room, where Emily was just finishing spreading everything out. She had brought up an armload of samples, as well as a bunch of notes.

"All right, I know this is a little chaotic, but we have a lot of things that we've been working on this week, and I can't wait to show you all of them," she said. She rubbed her hands together in excitement, and I couldn't help smiling at how adorable she was.

Then I shook my head. I needed to behave or I was going to do something that I regretted and make things harder than they needed to be. I cleared my throat. "All right, show me what you've got."

"Prepare to be impressed." Emily gave me a cocky smile that made me laugh.

As she went through her design modifications, though, the smile fell from my face, replaced with first a frown and then a slight scowl. I tried not to be frustrated with her. It was her first week on the job, and maybe she'd thought that my notes were more suggestions than anything else.

"We talked about this," I finally said, unable to help the exasperation that crept into my voice. It had been the same problem with the previous head designer, and the one before him. I knew what I wanted with the products, and it was my company. All Emily had to do was adhere to the brief. It seemed like that was too much for her, though.

Maybe I *had* made a mistake in hiring her. She clearly thought that we were close enough that she could take certain liberties. I doubted she would have tried something like that with anyone else.

"I know we talked about it," Emily said, "and you had some great ideas. But you have to realize that some of them just won't work."

"Excuse me?" I asked in disbelief.

Emily sighed. "Look, Patrick, I have to level with you, a lot of what you want just isn't practical. For example—"

"Aren't you the one who told me when I hired you that you have no experience in the outdoor industry?" I interrupted before I could help myself.

I hated the hurt look on her face, hated that I had been the one to cause it, but what right did she have to tell me that my ideas wouldn't work? I had been at this for a lot longer than she had. She might have fashion experience, but she didn't have experience in the industry.

I knew, even as I was thinking it, that none of my thoughts about Emily were even remotely fair. She had wanted to go into fashion for as long as I could remember, and even though she hadn't graduated yet, I knew that she had some great internships under her belt. Not only that, but I had been asking for a huge favor when I asked her to step in and work here.

She was just back in Saratoga Springs to deal with family stuff, and I had roped her into something else entirely, knowing that she was vulnerable because she probably needed the money and a distraction. Besides that, I had told her when she took the job that part of why she would do great at it was because we didn't want to appeal to just people like me who thought they had experience in the industry.

At the end of the day, if Emily was making suggestions, it wasn't because she was trying to stomp all over my expertise and my ideas. She was doing it because she genuinely was trying to help me make the business a success.

That realization didn't help calm me down now, though.

"Emily, if I'd wanted your input, then I would have asked for your input," I told her.

She bristled. "Look, maybe I'm not your target demographic," she said. "I know people, though. Even people who love the outdoors still want to be somewhat fashionable, in their own way. Your emphasis on function is great and all, but it leaves a lot to be desired. There's a such thing as wearability, you know!"

I bristled as well, and the next thing I knew, we were both nearly shouting at one another right there in the conference room.

*Oh no,* I thought miserably. It was as though I could see the room from a third-party point of view. I saw myself open my mouth, and I knew I was about to say something dumb. But I couldn't stop it. Instead, I barreled on, even as Emily's face tightened up with unhappiness.

I had never felt as guilty as I did right then.

# CHAPTER 15

## EMILY

Somehow, I had expected that when I showed Patrick my ideas, he would be excited about them. I had been working so hard all week, pulling so many late nights. For this? To have him yell at me for ignoring his notes? To have him throw back in my face all the insecurities that I'd had when I first took this job? Insecurities that he had told me to ignore?

I knew that I wasn't the right fit for the position. I didn't have experience in the outdoor industry, and I wasn't ready to take on something like it before I had even graduated, no matter how much experience I'd gotten at my previous internships. Head designer was a big deal. It was something that I had expected to work up to over the course of a decade or so with a company. Not something that I'd expected to just be handed.

That made me feel guilty. I had spent my whole life being handed opportunities. Now, here was another opportunity that I had been handed, when everyone else had to work for these sorts of things. Now, when everything else in my life was falling apart, it felt like a punch to the gut, more than anything else.

Especially now that it was obvious that Patrick hadn't hired me for my talent. He had only given me the job because he felt sorry for me because of my family's financial situation. Because he realized that I needed work, and he needed someone who would do as they were told, no questions asked.

I was surprised that Patrick thought that I would. Didn't he know me better than that? I wasn't exactly the poster child for doing exactly what people wanted me to do. That wasn't me.

Then again, Patrick barely knew me anymore. Sure, we had history. But we hadn't seen one another in nearly a decade now. Maybe he had forgotten.

"I didn't hire you to make suggestions," Patrick was saying. "I hired you to execute my vision. Not to change everything around and ignore my requirements."

I winced, ducking my head. I was upset that he wasn't willing to listen to me, but it was more than that. He had phrased this as a big opportunity for me, and I knew that he was right. In more ways than one. I needed the money, but I needed the experience as well. Especially if I wasn't going to have my parents' financial backing to launch my own fashion line. Especially if I wasn't even going to have the chance to finish my degree.

Had I screwed all of that up? I had thought that he would welcome my insights into the project. I had thought that he hired me because he knew that I was talented. But now, I had to admit that I was very worried that he was going to fire me on the spot.

The way that we were yelling at one another definitely didn't make my job feel any safer.

Trouble was, even though I knew that fighting with him over this was a surefire way to lose my job, I couldn't help but feel frustrated as well. I knew that what he wanted was never going to sell, not even to his supposed client base. That meant that by working on this project, I was wasting my time, potentially damaging my reputation as a designer. Didn't he see that?

So as much as I knew that this shouting match wasn't productive, I also knew that there had to be some way that I could get him to see sense.

"Hold on," I finally said, realizing I knew what the answer was. I was out of the room before he could react. I really hoped that he would still be there when I got back. I flew down the flight of stairs to the design floor and sprinted into the wardrobe closet, grabbing the older versions of the prototypes that had been put together before I joined the team.

Of course, they weren't 100% done to Patrick's standards either, but I hoped that I could show how my own prototypes offered him the best of both worlds. They drew on his designs, even matched them up to a certain point. There were some cosmetic changes, but they were a far cry from these other designs.

Would Patrick even listen to me about that, though? Or did he have his head far enough up his ass that he wouldn't even be waiting for me by the time I got back to the conference room?

Did I still have a job?

"All right," I said, coming back into the room. Patrick was standing at the window, staring out over Saratoga Springs. He turned when I came back. The look on his face was unreadable, but he wasn't yelling again. Yet.

I laid out two of the older prototypes, knowing that they

were closest to Patrick's vision. Slowly, I started to explain to him why I didn't think that they were marketable. Not that I would say that in so many words, but... Ugh. From the fabric to the shaping to the miniscule pockets, there were so many things that I'd like to change.

It took a while to explain all of that to Patrick, but slowly, I could see dawning comprehension in his face. *Yes!*

"Okay," he finally said, holding up a hand and cutting me off mid-sentence. He smiled ruefully as I trailed off. "Maybe there are certain modifications that my designs need. Like the pockets thing." He paused. "What are you thinking in terms of fabrics, though? I get that this one isn't the most comfortable, but we need something durable. Rugged. Weatherproof."

I nodded. "I know that," I said. "I've done a lot of research into our options this week. Unfortunately, I don't have many samples yet, but here are some ideas."

We started brainstorming, going from materials to overall design. I had forgotten what it was like to see Patrick like that; full of single-minded focus, passionate, intense in the best of ways. The next thing we knew, Faith was knocking on the door, raising an eyebrow at her boss.

"Just wanted to let you know that it's after five o'clock," she said, looking back and forth between the two of us.

I wondered if she suspected we were up to something other than brainstorming. Patrick's hair was messy from the way that he kept running his hands through it, his cheeks were slightly flushed with excitement.

The sketchbook on the table in front of him told the real picture, though. I honestly couldn't believe how adept his drawings were for someone who was 'just an athlete' and didn't know much about design. I'd need to come up with master copies of the design sheets eventually, but Patrick was giving me a lot to go on now that he was willing to compromise.

"Is it really after five?" Patrick asked, staring in surprise at his watch.

"It really is," Faith said, the corners of her mouth twitching into a smile. "I just wanted to let you know that I'm heading home. Unless you need anything else?"

"No, go ahead," Patrick said, waving her off. "We're just finishing up a little brainstorming on these things and then we'll be out of here as well. Have a great weekend, Faith, and I'll see you on Monday."

Faith nodded, but Patrick was already staring back at his sketchbook, quickly scrawling down another idea for himself. "How about this?" he asked me a minute later, spinning the sketchbook toward me. Suddenly, he looked up at me, his blue eyes piercing. "And please don't feel like you have to stay late, either." He rubbed the back of his neck with his hand. "I know I can be a little overwhelming when I'm chewing on an idea, but I also know that you have other projects in your life at the moment."

The movers were scheduled to come through that weekend, and everything had to be in boxes and ready to go by then. We would end up paying extra otherwise, since they worked on an hourly rate.

But suddenly, I wasn't worried about packing up the house. There was still a long way to go, but I'd figure it out somehow. Right now, there was nothing anyone could have done to tear me away from the conference room.

"I like this idea," I said, tapping on the sketchbook. It was an adjustment to one of my modifications, but it was almost brilliant. Almost. "But what about more something like this?" I leaned over him, my pencil ready, and started sketching up my own changes to adjust the design.

I couldn't get over what this felt like. We were a team, and we were working together. Harnessing our passion, our combined talents, focusing on something that interested us both. We were *creating* something, Patrick and I. Whoever would have thought we could ever get comfortable with one another again, let alone comfortable enough to create something like this?

Patrick watched my pencil dance across the paper for a moment and then turned toward me in his chair. It was only then that I realized how close we were. Close enough that I could see the gold flecks in those blue eyes of his, close enough that I could smell his spicy cologne, close enough that I could practically hear his heartbeat.

Tension sizzled between us. If it were a movie, the music would have hit a crescendo as we were silhouetted there in profile, just staring at one another. As it was, I could see the hunger in Patrick's eyes, and I knew that there was an answering hunger in my own.

I didn't know who moved first, but the next thing I knew, we were kissing again. I slid out of my seat, desperate to be closer to him, and ended up straddling his lap, my arms wrapped around his neck as his own fingers grasped my hips to steady me.

The kiss was practically desperate, our lips moving greedily against one another's, our tongues fighting a fierce battle for dominance. All of the passion, all of the tension, all of those feelings that we had locked away for the past decade rose to the surface again. I moaned with the intensity of it, goosebumps erupting across my skin as Patrick's fingers slid across my lower back.

I knew there were reasons that we shouldn't be doing this, but I couldn't think of a single one of them right then. There was just Patrick and me, his body moving against mine. We had always fit together perfectly before, and now was no exception.

I could feel how hard he was through his jeans, and I couldn't stop myself from grinding down against him, pressing my core down against his bulge. I turned breathlessly away from the kiss but made no move to pull away.

Patrick growled low in his throat and lifted me up, laying me down on the conference room table, right on top of all those various prototypes. Neither of us were thinking of work.

His fingers caught my panties and tugged them down, letting them fall carelessly to the floor. Then he tugged me closer to the edge of the table and knelt down, sealing his mouth to my lush folds. His tongue delved inside of me as his fingers stroked across my clit. I arched off the table, biting back a moan. Just because Faith had left for the day, it didn't mean everyone else had.

I couldn't think about the potential consequences of it, though. All I could think about was Patrick's hands on my body and his mouth between my legs. I gave myself over to the sensation.

I could still barely believe that it was happening again, that he still wanted me, after all these years. Our connection was still there, in spite of everything that I might have done to sabotage it, once upon a time.

It felt amazing to be with him again. I suddenly realized what the rest of my relationships had always been missing.

Patrick knew me better than anyone else ever could. He was my first, and he was the only man that I had ever truly let into my heart. It would be impossible to ever feel this way about anyone else.

Was I in over my head? As Patrick stood up, unbuttoning his pants, still between my legs, I knew that I was. I was in way over my head. But there was something altogether thrilling about that.

# CHAPTER 16

## PATRICK

I knew I shouldn't be doing this. I had promised Emily that I would keep things strictly professional between us after that first kiss. But I couldn't help getting caught up in the moment. Working together with her felt so natural. She really knew what she was doing when it came to design. At first, I had been frustrated at the way that she had changed all my designs without even consulting me. But now, I could see the reasons that she had done that.

Not only that, but she was willing to discuss things with me and make them even better. It felt like we could really do well together. Like we could create something great.

That was a heady feeling.

I had spent the whole afternoon trying not to think too hard about our close proximity or how much I'd like to ask her out to dinner after work. I'd tried to focus on the project. Fortunately, I tended to have a pretty single-minded focus when it came to my work, especially when it was something this important.

That didn't stop me from catching a whiff of her vanilla perfume every once in a while, or feeling a wave of lust go through me as our fingertips brushed against one another's while we discussed the prototypes that she had brought me.

I couldn't stop wanting her. It was impossible. She was just too smart, too sexy, too confident in what she was doing. I wasn't sure that I had ever seen Emily look this confident before. Maybe it was because it was just her and me, two old friends. Or maybe design school really had brought her out of her shell. She had always come up with great designs and drawings in high school, but it had taken so much coaxing to get her to share them with anyone.

Now she seemed to have figured out that confidence issue. And that in itself was sexier than I could believe.

When she turned toward me, our faces inches apart, I found myself holding my breath, waiting for her to move. I could see a hunger in her eyes, and I knew she wanted me just as badly as I wanted her. But she had pulled away from me before.

She hadn't pulled away this time. I didn't know if I had kissed her or she kissed me, but the next thing I'd known, we'd been tangled together on my chair, messily making out. Distantly, I'd known that I should stop it right here.

But where was the harm in kissing?

The harm was that it didn't stop there. We made out for what felt like forever. Then she ground down against me, her skirt all rucked up so that the only thing between her pretty pink pussy and my needy bulge was the thin fabric of her panties and my zipper.

It was clear that she had never stopped wanting me, any more than I had stopped wanting her.

The next thing I knew, I had her spread out on the conference room table and was licking and sucking my way along her quivering lady parts. Her sweet little noises went straight to my groin, making it impossible to think of anything outside of this moment. All I wanted in the world, right then, was to pleasure her.

I knew that she was trying to be quiet, but from the way she arched and twisted against the table, I could tell just how overwhelmed by sensation she was. That was furthered as I stood up, stroking myself to full hardness before pushing inside of her inch by slow inch. I held my breath as I paused, fully sheathed inside of her. Her body was hot and slick around my cock, and it was all I could do not to blow my load right then.

I finally managed to take a deep breath, calming myself down some. Emily grinned up at me, and I knew she could tell how close I was. She didn't tease me for it, though. Instead, she caught my hand, twisting her fingers in mine.

I started to move, slowly pulling out of her and then pushing back in. I picked up the pace a little, listening to her gasp, watching as her head tilted back and her eyes fluttered shut. I had forgotten how expressive she was during sex. Or maybe I'd thought that it was just her lack of experience that made every sensation seem so overwhelming to her. But she was just as easy to pleasure now as she had ever been.

She suddenly grabbed the edge of the table, using it for leverage so that she could meet me thrust for thrust. I could hear the crinkle of paper underneath her and realized distantly that we were probably destroying some of our hard work from that afternoon. But in that moment, I just couldn't find it in me to care. It was just Emily and me, and this moment.

Emily reached up and caught the lapels of my shirt, pulling me close to her. The angle was a little awkward as I tried to continue thrusting into her, but when she kissed me, I forgot all about that. My mouth moved hungrily against hers, drinking in her moans and delighting in the way that her fingers spasmed against my chest. She was getting close.

Good. I was too.

Neither of us lasted much longer, but it was still almost a surprise when my orgasm finally hit me, with all the force of a runaway train. I groaned and collapsed toward the table, barely managing to get my elbows out so that I didn't mash Emily back against the thing. I could feel her walls quaking around me, drawing out every last bit of my seed.

Eventually, our breathing returned to normal—and with it all of my concerns about what we had just done. I slowly let go of Emily and drew back, wondering what her expression would be. If she thought that I had crossed a line before, when all I had done was kiss her, what about now?

I felt ashamed. Of course I was attracted to her, but did I really have to act on it? It wasn't like I was a teenager anymore. I should have some sort of impulse control.

Sure enough, Emily was carefully not meeting my eyes, and from the faint flush on her face, I could tell that she was embarrassed about what had just happened. As soon as I pulled away, she jumped up, finding her underwear where I had carelessly tossed them on the floor. She pulled them on and tugged her skirt straight, fidgeting a little with her sleeves.

We had crossed a line, I realized. One that we couldn't ever uncross.

I tried to think of something to say to her. I didn't want to apologize, not for this. I wasn't sorry that it had happened, per se. Except that I had promised to keep things professional, and here I had just made love to her in the conference room, where who knew just who might walk in on us.

I was an idiot. I couldn't believe that I had just done that.

Emily was the first one to speak. "Patrick," she said slowly, "are you sure this is such a good idea?"

For a moment, I thought she was asking something else: was it such a good idea for us to resume our relationship? And maybe it wasn't. There was still that lingering hurt there from before. Not to mention all the other drama currently going on in her life, and the fact that I was trying to expand my business at the moment.

But maybe things could be better this time. We were both more mature and surer of ourselves. We knew what we wanted. We could figure out a way to make things work, I was sure of it.

That wasn't what Emily was asking, though. She finally looked up at me. "Me working for you," she clarified. "Is that such a good idea?"

I knew that she meant in light of what had just happened, but the idea of her not working for me was like a bucket of cold water thrown over me. I couldn't let her leave the company over this. I needed her.

I gestured toward the work that we had done that afternoon. Sure enough, some of the sheets were crumpled now, where they had been trapped beneath her body. They would need some cleaning up anyway. They were just rough drafts. I shouldn't be worried about them.

"Honestly, Emily, I've never been able to brainstorm with anyone like this before," I told her. "You understand what I want, and you always seem to know just how to make things better. Or at least, you're able to point out potential problems so that I can try to come up with a solution for them. I need you on my team."

"Okay," Emily said softly. "But are you sure that this is a

good idea? We just have so much history. This could interfere with the future of your company."

I sighed, understanding her concern. Jonah would probably have a fit if he found out that I was banging my new chief of design. He had already been skeptical when I hired Emily, citing her lack of experience. He had all but accused me of favoritism in giving her the job. This would be too much.

And as much as I had loved Emily, my company was everything that I had ever worked for. I couldn't just throw that away.

So instead, I said to her, "I know I told you that it would be strictly professional, and it will be from here on out. This was just a one-time thing. The chemistry was too good, and the pressure was too great to deny. Now we've got it out of our systems so that we can work without distraction."

Emily didn't look totally convinced, but finally she nodded. "If you're sure," she said.

"I'm sure," I told her. "This collaboration is going really well. I don't want to lose you. Just give it another shot. I promise I'll keep my hands to myself this time. Not to mention, I'll be going back to Boston soon enough and I'll be out of your hair."

"Okay," Emily said. She looked away from me again, this time to gather up the drawings and fold up the prototypes. I joined her at the table, but neither of us said anything.

I couldn't help feeling that we were both disappointed, but what else could I do?

# CHAPTER 17

## EMILY

Moving Mom and Dad into their new condo took most of the day Saturday, between getting the boxes moved out of the mansion and then organizing everything here. There was still too much stuff to comfortably fit in the condo, but I did the best I could, shoving some of the extra furnishings into the hall closet to be sorted through at a later date.

I was surprised when there was a knock at the door. Mom and Dad were out with friends who were hoping to cheer them up about the move, so I was there alone. For a moment, I debated not answering. After all, it wasn't my home. But finally, I decided to just do it.

Alyssa and Elliot stood there. The latter held up a bottle of wine. "We brought dinner," he said, looking proud of himself.

I laughed. "I don't think wine counts as dinner." Alyssa wordlessly held up the bag in her hands, and I could smell the scent of Chinese food wafting from it. "*Now* you're talking." I stepped back to let them in.

"We figured things were probably chaotic in here with

the move," Elliot said. He glanced around. "Oh wow, actually, this looks pretty great already."

"It's not a big space," I said, shrugging awkwardly. "Mom and Dad put a lot of their things in storage." I paused. "How did you figure out where the new place was, anyway?"

Alyssa gave me a look like, duh. "Saratoga Springs is not that big of a town," she reminded me. "You just have to know the right people, and you can find out anything that you want to know about anyone."

Of course. I was talking to the queen of gossip. If anyone was going to be able to figure out where my parents had moved to, Alyssa was the one. I had to admit, it was kind of good to have some company, even though I suspected that part of the reason they were there was to check out how low my family had sunk.

Alyssa cocked her head to the side as Elliot started doling out food in the kitchen and I worked on opening the wine. "So, are you going to be moving in here with them, or are you still living in New York?" she asked.

"Well, I'll be staying here for a little while since I'm working for Patrick's company at the moment," I said, shrugging. "But I'm not really living with them. I've still got my place in New York, and Patrick said that once I get familiar with the company, I can work remotely from there."

I thought about our meeting on the previous day, the part before he laid me out on a table and fucked me within an inch of my life. I tried not to blush as I thought about *that* part of the day.

It had been good working alongside him and bouncing ideas off one another. I wasn't sure that we would still be able to do that in the same way once I was in NYC again. Sure, technology had come pretty far, but it wasn't quite there yet to where we could be drawing on the same piece of paper as we scrawled down notes and ideas.

I pushed those thoughts aside. I wasn't staying in Saratoga Springs; that just wasn't an option. If I had to, I'd quit working for Patrick's company. It was that simple.

"Well, we have a surprise for you!" Alyssa said, grinning over at Elliot. "We're moving to the city too!"

I stared blankly at her. "Oh," I said in shock, not sure what to think about that announcement.

"You don't sound very surprised," Alyssa said.

"Oh, trust me, I'm surprised," I said. In all the time that I had lived there, Alyssa had only come to visit a couple times, sometimes dragging Elliot with her. I knew that she went shopping there occasionally, but I had never imagined that she would move there. In the city, she was one of a couple million rich girls, lost in the shuffle. In town, she was the "it girl", and she loved that attention.

"What brought this on?" I asked them.

Alyssa shrugged and flipped her hair back. "Saratoga Springs is getting kind of dull, you know?" she said. "I want a change of pace. I had to twist Elliot's arm to get him to agree to come with me, but it's going to be fun!"

I nodded, trying not to smile. I doubted she really had to twist Elliot's arm all that much. Once she decided that she wanted to move to NYC, he'd probably started packing. He wouldn't let her go without him, even if she continued to act oblivious to the fact that he had a crush on her.

"Well, that's cool," I said to her. "I guess we'll see a lot more of each other then."

"Yeah, it's going to be great," Alyssa said. "We're going to be sharing an apartment, so you can come over to ours all the time to hang out. It'll be so much fun."

I hummed in agreement. Of course, I doubted that they

were going to have to lift a finger to pay for said apartment. Their parents would probably be footing the bill for the rent. And they wouldn't be going to school. They'd have tons of time to explore the city and hang out and have fun. Meanwhile, I'd be working my butt off just to stay afloat.

Of course, when I thought about the work that I'd been doing this week, that didn't seem like such a terrible thing. Other than the start of that meeting with Patrick, where he had been so angry that I hadn't followed his design plans, everything had been great. This was the kind of job that I wanted to be doing, more than anything.

Well, maybe not more than anything. I still really wished that I could launch my own fashion line. But maybe if I worked hard enough and made enough connections, I could make that happen someday. I just hoped it wouldn't take me my whole life to work my way up.

"Have you already found a place?" I asked, trying not to sound too down on the idea of them moving to New York, even though I still didn't really understand why they wanted to.

"Yeah," Alyssa said. "And it's great. High ceilings, great views, huge bedrooms, and I think you could fit a whole orgy in the bathtub." She giggled, and I had to smile. "Anyway, it's super close to Patrick's new office there, so we can have lunch together all the time when you're working there."

I stared blankly at her. "Patrick's new office?" I asked.

Alyssa quirked an eyebrow at me. "Yeah, didn't he tell you about that?" she asked. "He's, like, moving the whole company to New York. He says it's something about, you know, opportunities and networking."

I continued to stare at her. How had Patrick failed to mention this to me? And he couldn't possibly be planning to move to NYC because of me, could he? We had said that things were going to be strictly professional between us, that the other day was just a one-time thing.

Then again, he had our future all planned out once before, and it had involved moving into an apartment together while we both went to school. Maybe this wasn't all that different. Maybe he was thinking that he could ease me into the idea by getting me to work for his company first and then convincing me to move back to New York with him.

I tried not to feel sick at the thought of it. This was probably just a happy coincidence. I just wasn't ready for anything serious. There was so much in my life that was already so screwy at the moment. Like this whole new condo that my parents had moved into, and the fact that I was going to have to work hard to keep an apartment of my own in NYC while my friends got to live the life that I had been living there before everything had gone to shit.

"I think it's going to be so great for Patrick to be in New York," Alyssa said. "I mean, I get that he had to go where he was drafted for hockey, but he's been in Boston for too long. He's just not a New England kind of guy, you know? And he, like, never got back to visit while he was there, so I think it'll be good for him to be in NYC. He can come visit his Saratoga Springs office more."

She beamed at me. "It's like we're all going to be together again, just like in high school!" she repeated enthusiastically.

I blinked at her, still trying to connect the dots. There was something that I was missing here. Suddenly, it seemed almost as though her moving to NYC had something to do with Patrick.

*Oh shit.*

Suddenly, the realization hit me like a ton of bricks: Alyssa had a big crush on Patrick back in school before I started dating him. I'd known all about it, actually, when Patrick asked me out. And given that Alyssa was my best friend, I probably should have said no to him, just out of principle.

But with the way that Patrick hounded me for a date, I thought it was pretty clear that he wasn't interested in Alyssa. Not only that, but I guess I'd just been more of a mean girl back then. I hadn't really cared about my friend's feelings.

Alyssa had gotten over her anger when she found out that Patrick and I were dating, and we'd managed to remain best friends. Did she think that I was out of the picture now, though?

The more I thought about it, the more jealous I felt of her.

*Wait, jealous?*

I supposed it made sense. Alyssa came on a little strong sometimes, but she was beautiful and witty. She still had her family's money too. She was basically getting to live the life that I'd just had ripped away from me.

"You okay?" Elliot asked suddenly, frowning at me. "You're kind of quiet tonight."

I shook my head, trying to clear it of those negative thoughts. "I'm just a little tired," I said. "This move has worn me out."

Elliot looked like he didn't quite believe me, but then he glanced over at Alyssa. Wisely enough, he let the matter drop. I forced myself to try to have fun with my friends, but by the end of their visit, all I felt was drained.

# CHAPTER 18

## PATRICK

I'd spent the whole weekend thinking about Emily, but by the time I headed in to work on Monday morning, I had decided that it was best to act as though nothing had happened. I had promised her that it was just a one-time thing. I would be strictly professional from here on out—for real this time. I couldn't go back on that promise.

Even though it felt like way too much had happened between us, and like there was no way to pretend everything was normal.

The thing was, I wasn't solely thinking back to Friday evening in the office. I was thinking about the night that I took her virginity, going with her to the prom, that weekend that we went camping alone, and that awful night of graduation, when she'd broken up with me. Nothing had been normal between us for a very long time now. As hard as it was to act like she didn't mean anything to me, I was forced to remember just how much I truly loved her.

I was thinking about everything that had ever happened between us, but Friday night had been special too. Friday night was the kind of reconciliation that I had spent a decade dreaming about and believing would never happen. It was as if all the longing that I had felt during those long years alone had finally had an outlet.

I wished that I hadn't been so desperate, that I had been able to hold her in that moment for just a little while longer, shown her just how much I worshipped her body.

Jesus, what was wrong with me? Letting myself get sucked back into the orbit of a girl who had spit me out like I'd been nothing to her. But no, I could see in her eyes that she was different. I could see in the way that she looked at me now that she knew she'd made a mistake back then. But that didn't mean she wanted me now.

Given half the chance, I'd do it all again. But that meant making sure that I wasn't given that half a chance. Things had to stay strictly professional, and that meant I could only check up on Emily's work when we weren't alone.

I hadn't gotten the chance to meet with Emily the previous Friday afternoon. Or maybe it was more that I was afraid that if I saw her that day, a week after we'd had sex in the conference room, then I would do something stupid like ask her out to dinner. Even if Jonah was there during all of our meetings now, putting his trip back to Boston on hold temporarily while we discussed our options for New York.

He had originally protested his inclusion, until I reminded him that as a business partner, he needed to know just as much as I did about the line that we were planning on launching. He'd given me a look like he knew that wasn't the real reason I wanted him there, but after that, he at least had quit complaining about it.

I'd chatted with Emily and her team a few times the previous week for shorter meetings, and I knew that they had begun modifying the prototypes. But I was surprised when Emily walked into Monday's meeting with an armload of material. "Prototypes," she said, laying them out on the table. "I think we have one for pretty much every piece now. A couple still need slight modifications, but they're starting to really come along."

"I'll say," I said in surprise, running my fingers over one of the pieces.

"So," Emily said, clapping her hands together. "As you can see, we made a few more changes this week with some of the designs. For example, this one here." She walked us through all of the changes, and all I could do was nod along. Originally, I'd thought that I would come up with all of the designs and just have her execute what I wanted, but now, I had to admit that I was so glad that I had brought her on board. She had taken my ideas to the next level.

"What about changing the cut of this one?" Jonah asked, showing what he meant by folding the fabric a little.

Emily shook her head and giggled. "You're just like Patrick," she said. "Trust me on this one."

Jonah laughed. "Yeah, I guess I'm pretty fashion-illiterate," he agreed. "Especially when it comes to women's clothes."

"I mean, to be fair, some of Patrick's suggestions were even worse," Emily added, her eyes twinkling teasingly as she looked over at me.

"Hey!" I said, putting my hand over my heart and pretending offense.

She grinned wider and put a hand on my arm. "Don't worry, at least you'll always have your looks," she said. Then she paused dramatically. "At least for a few more years, anyway."

I snorted. Jonah was looking back and forth between the two of us, and I hurriedly pulled my arm away before he could realize just how familiar we were with one another. I still wondered what he suspected about our relationship, but I wasn't offering up any information if he wasn't asking for it.

I had to admit, just having her brush my arm like that sent a thrill through me. It was part of what made the whole project so exciting. I got to see Emily nearly every day, even if I couldn't be alone with her anymore. I had been excited about the apparel line before she came onboard, of course, but now, I couldn't wait to get it out into the stores and on our online catalogue.

Even after I stepped away from Emily, I noticed that Jonah was still looking at me funny. I cleared my throat. "We should probably leave Emily to her work," I said to him, trying not to sound guilty, even though that small touch had sent my desire into overdrive. I needed to get out of there before I did something stupid.

Jonah nodded. "Emily, let us know when those prototypes are all finished," he said.

From the way that Emily was looking at me, I could tell that she sensed the awkwardness in the room. Fortunately, she simply gathered up the things that she had brought into the meeting and headed back to her office to chat with the rest of the design team.

"We should talk about how best to introduce the retailers to this line," I said to Jonah as we headed down the hall toward our own offices.

Jonah nodded, but he seemed distracted. He shut the door carefully behind us. "Patrick, you know this isn't working," he said quietly, taking a seat across from my desk.

I raised an eyebrow at him. "What do you mean?" I asked. "You don't like the line? I know that Emily vetoed a few of your suggestions today. She's done that with some of mine as well. But I think she's right about the things that she says." I paused. "I know you're still not sure about her qualifications or any of that, but seriously, I think she's going to take this line to the next level."

Jonah shook his head. "It's not about her vetoing suggestions, or her qualifications," he said. "Look, I know you guys have a history. I don't know what that entails, but it's pretty obvious to anyone who's in the room with you for more than a couple of minutes that it wasn't strictly platonic." He paused. "It's affecting your ability to work together. Don't try to deny it."

I raised an eyebrow at him. "What, you don't think I'm being hard enough on her? Not demanding the best? You think she's getting away with not giving me her everything? Do you know how many late nights she's pulled since she started working here? I swear she has to be one of the last people in the office every night."

I didn't mean to sound so defensive about her, and to be honest, I didn't know exactly what Jonah was implying. I wasn't going to just sit by and let him attack Emily, though. She was doing an amazing job, even better than I could have expected.

Jonah rolled his eyes. "It has nothing to do with her work, per se," he said. "It's not lost on me though that the only reason you have me in these meetings is to babysit the two of you. That's not my job. And I have plenty of other things that I need to do for this business other than sit there in your meetings, like getting back to Boston."

"That's not why I asked you to be there," I protested, wondering if he could hear the lie for what it was. "You're my business partner. You're going to help me shop this line around to different retailers. And that means you need to know the progress that we're making with it."

"No, it means I need to see the final product," Jonah

said firmly. "As we talked about in today's meeting, I'm even less capable of figuring out the fashion stuff than you are. There's a reason I work the numbers and schedule the meetings. That's my job. Your job is to oversee product development. You don't need me there for that."

I was silent for a long moment, feeling chastised. I knew that he was right.

"There's a reason," Jonah added, his tone significant, "that you didn't seem to need me in these meetings until it was Emily that was your head designer."

I sighed. "We do have a history," I finally said. "And yes, I am attracted to her. But things are strictly professional between the two of us. As much as I'd like to say that I'll take your reservations into consideration and try to find another head designer, the fact remains that work on this new line is going gangbusters since she got here. We haven't had this much progress in months. I thought you were the one who was so worried about hitting our deadlines."

"I am," Jonah sighed. He still looked doubtful. "I don't know, Patrick. I've never seen you this way around a woman before, that's all. You're not really doing anything to hide it from me or anyone else either. Although I understand that you two have a history, I just hope you remember that if there's any sort of scandal, it could affect the future of the company. This is not the day and age to be playing around like that, even if it is fully consensual."

I grimaced and stared at my desk. "Well, there's nothing happening," I assured him. "Nor will anything happen in the future."

Jonah looked like he didn't fully believe me, but he let the matter lie. I just hoped that I could keep my word to both of them and refuse to allow anything unprofessional to happen again.

# CHAPTER 19

## EMILY

I couldn't accuse Patrick of avoiding me. He saw me nearly every day, checking up on the progress with the new apparel line and the prototypes that my team were furiously putting together. He made a few suggestions here and there, but for the most part, he seemed to have gained a lot more confidence in the changes that I made to his basic designs.

I had to wonder if that had anything to do with him not wanting to criticize me too much—especially not in front of everyone else.

And there were always other people around. That was what made the whole thing so strange. I couldn't accuse him of avoiding me, but at the same time, I never saw him alone again after we'd had sex in the conference room. Either Jonah was there, or the designers were there, or his secretary was there. Someone was always there babysitting us.

That was probably a good thing. I couldn't seem to quit thinking about him. I couldn't seem to quit dreaming about him. I wanted to say that I wouldn't try anything unprofessional if I saw him alone, but I didn't know if I had the willpower to hold myself back.

I kept thinking about how Alyssa might be interested in him, and how much of a catch he clearly was for anyone else. I couldn't help feeling jealous. I wanted him back.

But he was my boss. And I'd broken his heart.

The other challenge with never catching him alone was the fact that I still needed to ask him about New York City and the supposed move to an office there. I couldn't stop thinking about what Alyssa had said. I wondered how she knew about the move before any of his employees seemed to. This was Alyssa, though. She always seemed to know what the good gossip was, and Patrick's search for real estate in New York City wouldn't have gone under the radar.

Why was he moving to NYC, though? And why hadn't he told me?

It was all so confusing. I tried not to think about it, instead choosing to focus on the prototypes to the exclusion of pretty much everything else.

Except that now, those prototypes were finished.

"I have to admit, I'm impressed," Jonah said, which was about the highest praise that I could receive. I wasn't sure exactly what the deal was or what Patrick might have told him, but I'd gotten the distinct feeling that the man either didn't particularly like me or didn't like my work. He smiled at me now, though, then turned to Patrick. "We're going to have our pick of retailers."

Patrick nodded. "I know," he said, enthusiasm in his voice. He put an arm around my shoulders and gave me a quick, one-armed hug. "Seriously, Emily, thanks for all your work. This is so much better than I could have expected. I mean, these are just the prototypes, and already they look totally professional and like something you could buy in a store."

I grinned at him, trying not to blush too hard. *It's the praise, not the hug,* I told myself, even though I knew that was only partially true. "So, what happens next?"

"Well actually, I was really hoping that we would get this all done by Friday because Jonah's actually scheduled a photoshoot for this weekend at Niagara Falls," Patrick said, sounding pleased.

I stared at him in horror. "You didn't tell me that!" I said. "What if I hadn't gotten everything done in time?"

Patrick shrugged, not looking concerned. "You managed to sew me into a jockey uniform at a moment's notice, using scraps from your high school prom dress," he joked. "I was pretty sure we could pull something off."

I had to laugh at that. "All right, fair enough," I said. "So, a photoshoot at Niagara Falls?"

"Yeah," Patrick said. "We're hoping to generate a little interest in the line prior to going to the manufacturer so that we can estimate demand."

"It'll also give us a bit of a bargaining chip when it comes to shopping around for a retailer," Jonah added. "If we can show them how much interest we've already generated, chances are we'll be more likely to be picked up by someone who can really sell the product for us."

"Sure," I said, nodding. "Honestly, though, I doubt you're going to have to work too hard to sell these." I fingered one of the jackets that we had designed. It was waterproof and windproof and packed down to next to nothing. Plus, it came with a whole host of other perks that made it great for travel.

"We're actually headed up to Niagara Falls this afternoon to meet with the photography team," Patrick added. "I know it's short notice because I didn't want to stress you out before, but we were really hoping that you could come along with us, just in case we need any modifications to the prototypes once we're on the ground there."

I frowned at him. "It's more than short notice," I said. But it wasn't like I was doing anything else with my life at the moment. And maybe while we were in Niagara Falls, I'd have a chance to finally catch him on his own and ask him about the NYC plans.

"I'll need to go home and pack," I said. "Are we going to be there all weekend?"

"That's the plan," Patrick affirmed, nodding. "If you can't do it, I'm sure one of the other designers can. We actually already talked to Sarah about it."

I snorted. "Are you trying to tell me that you've been undermining my authority with my team?" I teased.

"Got me," Patrick said, grinning easily. Jonah rolled his eyes but didn't comment. "Go on home and pack. I'll pick you up in a little while on the way to the airport. Sound like a plan?"

"Sure," I said. "I'll see you in a bit."

A couple hours later, we were on our way to Niagara Falls on Patrick's private jet. I couldn't get over how successful he was. I remembered that beat-up old pickup truck that he used to drive in high school. Those years seemed like a lifetime ago now. I couldn't believe how wrong I had been about him.

Look at him now.

Indeed, look at him now. He was sitting up front in the copilot's seat, helping navigate. Somehow in the ten years since I had last seen him, he'd had a successful athletic career, built a business, learned how to pilot planes, and then some. But that wasn't what attracted me to him. In fact, it was just the opposite. It was the fact that he was still the same guy despite all of his successes.

As though he was able to read my thoughts, Patrick suddenly turned around to grin at me from over his shoulder. He winked as though to say, *pretty cool, huh?*

The surprises didn't stop there. When we got to Niagara Falls, we headed to the hotel. I couldn't help but feel wowed by the suite that I was shown to. If Patrick was trying to impress me, he'd certainly done the job right. I understood why he wanted me there to help with the photoshoot.

Still, it seemed a little excessive. I was glad that I had dug through my closet and found a few really nice outfits to wear. I showered and put on a pretty black dress before heading down to dinner at the hotel's restaurant. Patrick was there waiting by the door, his tongue between his teeth as he composed a message on his phone.

"Hey," I said.

Patrick looked up, his expression breaking into a smile. "Wow, you look amazing," he said, giving me a heated once-over that made me flush with desire. But no, that wasn't what this weekend was about. Especially not this evening, when we were meeting Jonah and the photographers for dinner.

"How's the room?" he asked me.

I raised an eyebrow at him. "Huge, actually," I said. "You didn't have to get me a suite, you know."

Patrick shrugged. "Jonah and I are in a suite," he said. "It didn't feel right not getting one for you too. I didn't think you'd want to share with us."

I had to laugh. "Jonah would have vetoed that, I think," I said. I paused. "Does he know—" Before I could finish that question, Jonah appeared with three other men. I recognized two of them from the previous photoshoot. "Hey," I said. "It's Matt, right?"

Matt beamed at me and shook my hand. "It's our wardrobe fixer extraordinaire," he said. "Patrick, I'm so glad you brought her along again. This time, no way in hell are we losing the light."

We all laughed and headed into the restaurant. The first part of the evening was all business talk. It turned out that only one of the men with Matt was his assistant photographer. The other man worked for one of the retailers who might be interested in Patrick's line. I listened as they chatted about the specifics, even though none of it really pertained to me.

It just gave me even more of an appreciation for Patrick the businessman.

As the night wore on, the business talk seemed to be winding down. Finally, Jonah ordered a couple bottles of champagne to be brought to the table. "To new beginnings," he toasted.

"Hear, hear," Patrick said, and we all took a drink.

We quickly polished off a couple bottles, coming up with more and more outlandish toasts as we went. Another bottle was ordered, then another. Finally, when we were all a bit tipsy, the men all shook hands and headed their separate ways.

When it was just the three of us in the hallway, Patrick turned to Jonah and gave him a huge hug. "We did it," he said, sounding proud.

To my surprise, Jonah reached out and snagged me, pulling me into the hug. "We did it," he agreed. He broke away. "All right, those drinks were for them. Let's head to the bar."

Patrick snorted. "Amen," he said. "God, I hate champagne."

"You couldn't tell from the way you kept knocking it back," Jonah teased.

"Oh, you could," I chimed in. "All you had to do was look at the pained expression on his face. He gets all puckery around the mouth every time someone makes him drink champagne." I couldn't help admitting that I had been watching Patrick all night, thinking about how there were some things that would probably never change.

He nudged me with his shoulder. "I never hated champagne until that time we stole the bottle from your parents' basement," he said.

"You only hated that bottle because we knocked the cork into it and had to strain out all the little pieces as we drank it," I reminded him. "Or that's what you told me anyway."

"I was trying to be macho," Patrick said.

"Macho men don't love to drink champagne, last I heard," Jonah laughed.

"Yeah, well, they do at all the sporting events," Patrick reminded him. "Worst champagne I've ever had was when we won nationals in college. We were downing it out of the championship cup and oh boy. Worst hangover I've ever had, too."

"It was probably cheap," Jonah said with a shrug.

"I couldn't tell the difference," Patrick said.

I sat back, watching the two of them banter for a bit. I still didn't know how they had met or become business partners, I realized. But I could tell that they were good friends. They joked easily with one another, like they had been best friends for years.

Alyssa was my best friend, but we had never been *that*

close to one another. I suddenly wondered if we really were best friends, or if it was just that we had known one another forever now. From there, my thoughts turned gloomy. The same thing could hold true for Patrick and me; were we really friends at this point? I didn't know anything about him, really. Not even that he planned on moving his business to NYC.

Ten years was a long time to go without speaking. I had really messed up everything when I broke up with him.

It was hard to stay melancholy for long, though, with Jonah and Patrick cracking increasingly hilarious jokes. We ordered drinks, and before long, I found myself smiling and laughing along, having a great time.

There was a lot that I wanted to ask Patrick about, starting with the New York office and ending with whether or not I still had a job now that all the prototypes were finished. But tonight was just about celebrating and having a little fun.

I didn't want it to end.

Jonah started yawning around midnight, and the two of us found ourselves yawning too. "All right, I'm headed to bed," he said, standing up as he drained the last of his drink. "We've got a long day tomorrow."

"He says after we've mixed three different kinds of drinks," Patrick stage-whispered to me, and I giggled.

Jonah rolled his eyes fondly. "Oh, come on, Patrick. You've got enough of the Scotch/Irish blood in you that we all know you'll look like a ray of sunshine in the morning while everyone else is dying," he said.

Patrick puffed up his chest. "I do have superior genes," he boasted, and we all laughed. He fist-bumped his business partner. "See you tomorrow," he said. "I'm going to finish up this drink before I go, and I don't feel like chugging it."

"Probably wise," Jonah agreed. He turned and headed for the elevators. Then it was just Patrick and me.

"I should probably head to bed as well," I sighed. To be honest, I felt pretty wired still, both from the excitement and from the sheer proximity of Patrick. I wasn't sure that I should be sitting alone with him in a bar.

"Oh, come on," Patrick said, his eyes glinting with a challenge. "You've been slow on your drinks all night. You can afford to have another. Don't leave me drinking alone!"

I laughed and slowly sank back into my seat. "All right, all right," I said. "I'll have another one. Only because you're right, it wouldn't be nice to leave you drinking by yourself."

I flagged down the bartender and ordered another drink.

# CHAPTER 20

## PATRICK

When Jonah went up to bed, I could hear the faintest sound of alarm bells in the back of my head. I was a little too tipsy to trust myself with Emily. On the other hand, I was enjoying myself too much to want to let her go up to bed as well. I sipped slowly at my drink as the conversation turned to Saratoga Springs and some of the people we knew who still lived there.

We were careful not to talk about *us* in high school, but I could tell that we were both thinking about it. Especially when she brought up Alyssa. "You know, she had the biggest crush on you," Emily said. Then she clapped a hand over her mouth. "I wasn't supposed to tell you that."

I laughed. "I already knew," I said dismissively, waving it away. "I think she still does, actually. Not interested, though. Never have been."

"Good," Emily said with surprising vehemence.

"Poor Elliot," I said, not sure what else to say.

Emily snickered. "Poor Elliot," she agreed. She paused. "They're moving to New York City. They said you're opening an office there."

I blinked in surprise. "Yeah, how did... Oh. Right. Alyssa."

"Alyssa," Emily agreed, sighing. "So, it's true?"

"We've been thinking about opening an office there for a while now," I said, hoping she didn't feel weird about it. "Before you started working for us. It's just, we bought this other company and their office is there. It's more just the personnel. I haven't decided exactly what I want to do yet."

"Oh," Emily said, looking relieved. "That makes a lot of sense."

"You thought I was moving just to be with you?" I teased. I regretted the words the minute they were out of my mouth. Emily looked off to the side and shrugged, and I couldn't tell if she was embarrassed or upset.

"Come on," I said, getting to my feet. "Let's go for a walk to clear our heads." I knew that what we actually should be doing was heading upstairs to bed. It wasn't like we were going to have sex in an alleyway, though. As long as we were out in public, I could enjoy her company without worry.

"Good idea," Emily said, getting to her feet as well.

We were both a little wobbly as we walked around town. It was getting late, but there were a surprising number of places that were still open. Well, maybe not too surprising, it was a tourist town, after all.

One of the places that still had all its lights on was a little wedding chapel. I snickered as I saw the neon sign flashing two interconnected hearts. "How funny would it be if we ended up getting married, after everything that's happened between us?"

Emily laughed. "It would definitely be ironic," she said. "Especially since I was such an asshole to you back then and look how the tables have turned. I'm surprised you've been so nice to me to be honest with you."

I shrugged. "We were kids, Emily. Dumb kids who didn't know any better." I tried to blow it off, but now that I had the idea in my head, it refused to go away.

Would it be so bad, marrying Emily? I had loved her, and I was pretty sure that she had loved me. In spite of everything that had happened, in spite of the breakup, there we were, drawn inexplicably together again. It had to be a sign, didn't it, that after ten years we were still just as into one another as we had been before?

"Come on," I said, grabbing her hand and dragging her toward the chapel. "Let's go inside. Just to see what it looks like."

Emily shook her head. "You're crazy," she said, but she was smiling fondly at me, and she followed me inside, just drunk enough to give it a shot.

We stumbled in, and it was just as cheesy on the inside as it was on the outside, with fake flowers everywhere and lots of kitschy souvenirs that you could buy after your wedding.

There was a nice elderly woman behind the counter. "Are you two here to get married?" she asked, looking back and forth between us. Without waiting for a reply, she twitched aside a curtain, calling into the back room, "Barry, I need you!"

"You always need me," said the cute old man as he appeared behind her.

"That I do," she said, leaning into his side. The two of them were so easy with one another, like they knew exactly where they belonged. Like they'd had a lifetime to get comfortable with one another.

But you could spend a whole lifetime with someone and

not get that. I knew because I could never seem to get comfortable with anyone other than Emily. Suddenly, I wanted that for us.

"I like to ask some questions before I agree to marry a couple," Barry said seriously. "The divorce rate these days, my lord. Now, have you two lovebirds been together for long?"

"We're high school sweethearts," Emily said, giggling a little as she looked up at me. Suddenly, I could see the way that we looked from the outside. Like we were really in love. But Emily didn't stop there. "I always thought we'd be married just out of school, but then there was the tragedy that kept us apart for years."

"The tragedy, eh?" the old woman asked.

"Margaret, don't pry!" Barry hissed.

I smiled at them. "It's all right," I said. "All my love is saying is that there was a thing with her aunt. She didn't think we were ready to get married yet."

"And so she kept us apart for a decade!" Emily declared, her eyes twinkling as she looked up at me. "She was actually in love with you herself. That's why she was against the marriage!"

Barry and Margaret looked shocked. I tried not to snicker. "Aunt Lily had a thing for me? You never told me!"

"Well, what if you had run off with her instead?" Emily asked, putting a hand over her heart. "I just wouldn't have been able to bear it, Pattycakes." She turned to Margaret. "We all know how men prefer a woman with experience, and we were so young back then."

"Mm-hmm," Margaret said, but even though the story was ludicrous, she sounded like she was waiting to hear the ending.

"They sent you away to a nunnery," I sighed, as though

it really were a tragedy. "I didn't know that was even possible in this day and age. I looked and looked and looked for you, but I couldn't find any information. They covered their tracks well."

"But you found me in the end, and that's all that matters," Emily said firmly.

There were sighs from the other side of the counter.

"My family still isn't happy to hear that we've found one another again," Emily confessed to the chapel owners. "If they knew that we were here, they'd be sure to cut me off and we'd have to live off of Ramen noodles and boxed mac and cheese."

"If we can just get married, there won't be anything that they can do," I said. "Once you're married, the money is yours, right? That's how the trust is worded?"

Barry looked like he didn't know what to say. "I don't know if I should marry you just because you're worried she might lose her inheritance," he finally said. "Young lady, I'm not sure why your family doesn't wish for you to marry him, but perhaps it's for the best."

"Oh, Barry, they're high school sweethearts!" his wife protested. "We can't turn them away."

"They don't even have witnesses with them," Barry pointed out. "You need two witnesses to get married!"

Barely aware of what I was doing, I pulled out my wallet and dragged out two slightly crumpled hundred-dollar bills. "Would the twin Ben Franklins count?" I asked.

Barry laughed and shook his head, looking down at his wife.

"I'm sure we can find them some witnesses," Margaret said. "Oh, you remember what it was like for us! We wanted to get married when we were sixteen, but your family wouldn't let us. These two have been waiting quite long enough."

Barry finally relented. "All right," he said, reaching out and grabbing the bills. "We'll see what we can do. Margaret, why don't you help the lovely young bride get dressed?"

Margaret winked at Emily and led her away behind some curtains. I turned back toward Barry, but he had disappeared as well. And suddenly, I realized what I had done.

Were we actually getting married? Was that even legal?

But no, we couldn't possibly be actually getting married. Emily would have protested otherwise. We weren't even really a couple; we had just told them some lies for fun. That was it.

This wasn't real. That realization in itself was pretty funny. I was still grinning when Barry came back and led me into the chapel.

# CHAPTER 21

## EMILY

I giggled as I stood across from Patrick at the altar. Margaret had dressed me in a shockingly short white dress and an itchy veil, but Patrick was looking at me tenderly, as though I was the only person in the world that he would want to marry.

We were standing at the altar while a guy who looked like Santa Claus stood on one side and Margaret stood on the other. Barry started reading out the ceremony rites, and suddenly it hit me that we were really getting married. It wasn't just a joke; it was for real.

I looked up at Patrick, my eyes wide, and suddenly we both burst into laughter. No, this couldn't be real. We were standing next to goddamn Santa, after all. This whole thing was just a joke, from the story that we had told to Barry and Margaret to the rest of it. What had Patrick said as we were on our way in? Just to see what it would be like.

That was all.

When it came time for the vows, I simpered at him. "I promise to spend all your money and to sew you as many crazy designs as you want," I said.

Patrick snorted. "I vow to buy you the best sewing machine that money can buy, and this time if you're going to go bum around Europe for a year, I'm really coming with you. There's nothing that you can do to stop me."

"Ooh, Europe would be fun for the honeymoon," I said.

"It would," Patrick agreed.

Barry cleared his throat, reminding us that we were still in the middle of the ceremony. The next thing I knew, he was pronouncing us man and wife, and then we were kissing. The kiss was searing in its intensity, and I stumbled into Patrick, my legs feeling like jelly. Santa started to serenade us, and I had never had a more perfect moment in my life, I decided.

Getting back to the hotel room was all a blur, and I didn't really remember much of anything until Patrick and I were tumbling naked into the bed together. He pressed me back against the sheets, and I giggled, unable to help myself.

"What?" Patrick asked in a hushed tone.

"I just realized, I don't think we've ever had sex in a bed before," I whispered back. When we were teenagers, we had been sneaking around, trying to escape notice, having sex in his truck or on the couch in the basement of his parents' house, a couple times.

Patrick grinned and kissed my palm. "Then I'd better make this good," he said.

I laughed and spread my legs, letting him slide between them. "It's our wedding night," I reminded him. "You'd definitely better make this good."

Patrick laughed and claimed my mouth in a kiss.

# CHAPTER 22

## PATRICK

I lost myself in the feeling of being with Emily. Her body was warm against mine, her skin smooth as I trailed kisses down the length of her. I toyed with her breasts, teasing her until she was squirming and wordlessly begging for more. Slowly, I dragged one hand down her side and pressed my fingers between her legs, questing for that slick opening of hers.

She was already open and wanting, her body quivering with need for my hard prick. I pushed inside of her in one swift movement, kissing her again as I did so, swallowing her sweet moans.

Our bodies moved together as if we were one. As if that marriage had been real, and we truly were husband and wife now. I grinned against her mouth. Who knew that one day Emily and I would have a fake marriage and be serenaded by Santa?

I forgot about the little wedding chapel as I continued to kiss Emily more deeply. I knew I was probably still a little intoxicated, but I was drunk on her kisses more than anything else.

She held on tightly to me, pulling my body close against hers, and I wrapped my arms around her, continuing to kiss her as I rocked into her again and again. I could feel her body tense against mine as she turned her face to the side, gasping for breath as she trembled her way toward an orgasm. Still so delightfully responsive. What a wonderful woman.

I kissed her jaw and nipped at her earlobe, drawing a high and reedy sound from her lips. "Pat, please," she begged, and I groaned in response, thrusting ever harder into her heat.

As we both drew closer to release, our movements became more frenzied and a little bit sloppy. But still, it was somehow perfect. I could practically feel my love for her radiating out from my body, and when Emily looked up at me, I could see in her eyes that she still loved me too. I kissed her one last time as we both spilled over the brink, crying out each other's names, our fingers twisted into one another's.

We collapsed into bed, and I barely had the presence of mind to pull her close to me. I fell asleep almost immediately, my body nothing but warmly content.

The next morning, I woke up to my cellphone ringing shrilly. Groaning, I groped on the nightstand for it but didn't find it. I did, however, find a warm body sprawled against mine in the bed. *Emily*.

I pried my eyes open, smiling at her sleeping form for a moment before practically leaping out of bed. Emily. Shit.

I had promised her that everything would be strictly professional from here on out, and yet I hadn't even managed to go one night in Niagara Falls before I had tumbled into bed with her. But she'd been more than a willing participant.

Still, I shook my head and grabbed my pants, pulling out my phone. "Where the hell are you?" Jonah immediately asked. "I pounded on your door for ten minutes and then realized you weren't in there. Don't tell me you slept in Emily's room last night."

I looked at the time and swore under my breath. We were going to be late for the photoshoot. Not only that, but Jonah had made it very clear that he didn't think my relationship with Emily was a good idea.

"Go down to breakfast and I'll meet you in the lobby in half an hour."

"Damn it, Patrick," Jonah started to say. I hung up before I could hear anything else.

Emily sat up in bed, wiping sleepily at her eyes. "What's up?" she asked.

"Things got a little out of hand last night," I said sheepishly, wondering how much she remembered. My own memories were a little fuzzy, but we had definitely had sex, and that was something that I hadn't meant to do. Especially not while inebriated.

Emily, rather than looking upset, grinned crookedly at me. "A little out of hand," she agreed.

"We have thirty minutes to get down to the lobby before Jonah figures out something's up," I told her. I started yanking on my clothing. "For now, let's just focus on work, okay? This photoshoot and the line launch are a big deal for the company."

It was kind of an asshole thing to say because I was pretty sure that I had been the one to initiate last night, and now I was telling her to ignore it so that we could focus on the company. But she nodded anyway.

"Sure," she said. "I'll see you downstairs." Did she

sound slightly disappointed, or was that just wishful thinking? I didn't have time to dwell on it now, either way.

I finished getting dressed and all but raced back to my own suite. Jonah was nowhere to be seen, fortunately, or else he probably would have snidely asked me why I'd gone for a run wearing the same clothes that I'd had on the night before. I danced out of said clothes and took a quick shower, letting the hot water rush over my body.

It was as I was reaching for the faucet to turn the water off that I froze, staring down at my left hand. There was a small, tacky copper band on my ring finger, and suddenly the memories from last night came rushing back.

*Holy shit. Emily and I got married.*

# CHAPTER 23

## EMILY

I didn't think that I had ever gotten ready faster than I did that morning, but I still barely made it down to the lobby on time. I knew that I didn't look my best. My hair was already falling out of its ponytail, and my head was pounding from a hangover that no doubt had left shadows beneath my eyes. But the team was gathered, so I forced myself to focus on the task at hand. I just hoped they wouldn't need me to stitch together anything too important.

Patrick, of course, looked totally normal, just like Jonah had predicted. I wasn't the only person looking a bit rough, though, I realized. That made me feel a little better.

We headed out to do the photo shoot in a dramatic location near the falls. A male and female model met up with us at the designated site. I helped them into their outfits and then found a place to sit and watch the shoot, trying to ignore my throbbing headache. What the hell had Patrick and I even done the night before?

The only thing I knew for sure was that we'd had too much to drink and then apparently tumbled into bed together. I knew he wanted to stay focused on the shoot, and I knew that we both had a million other reasons not to get involved with one another at the moment, not least of which because he was my boss. But I couldn't regret what had happened the night before.

Even if I barely remembered it.

It was as Patrick was taking a sip of his coffee later that the light glinted just right off a thin copper band on his finger. I stared for a minute, suddenly remembering. I had picked that out for him at the gift shop, claiming that we had to have some way of remembering...what? What was it that we'd been doing?

I stared at the ring for just long enough for Patrick to see me looking. He grimaced and transferred his coffee to his other hand, shoving the one with the ring back into his pocket.

And suddenly, it hit me. That little chapel. The older couple. *Santa.* Had Patrick and I really gotten married the night before? I felt sick to my stomach just thinking about it, and this had nothing to do with the lingering nausea of a hangover.

I pushed those thoughts out of my mind and tried to focus on the shoot. I helped the models in and out of various outfits as the photographers worked to get the angles just right.

I was exhausted by the time we made it to a local restaurant for our celebration dinner.

I knew that I should be excited about the launch of the line. I had poured my heart and soul into this for the past few weeks. It sounded like things were really looking positive, too. The photographers were happy, and the businessmen were already talking the terms of the deal.

Instead of excitement, though, all I felt was confused and awkward. I kept glancing over at Patrick or noticing him glancing over at me. I wished that we could talk, but obviously we couldn't in front of everyone else.

It had just been a joke, right? I wouldn't have just gotten drunk and married Patrick.

Back in high school, I'd had a plan for my wedding. It would be a huge party, I would have a beautiful white dress, and everyone we loved would be there with me. I wouldn't have thrown away that fantasy to get married in a cheap mini dress in some tacky chapel in Niagara Falls, would I?

Even if we *had* actually gotten married, it wasn't legal, was it? We were both drunk. We hadn't meant it. And we hadn't filed for a license. No, it couldn't be legal.

Yet I found myself wondering if maybe there was some sliver of me that really wanted it to be. That was stupid though. We had barely even seen one another for the past decade. We were totally different people than we had once been. Even though the sex was still great, it was just sex. Just a one-time thing that...kept happening, somehow.

I couldn't deny, however, that my feelings for him still held true. I'd thought they had just been childish fantasy, but now I knew, they had been real and strong. And they were growing stronger by the day. I glanced over at Patrick again. Did he remember the wedding? I was sure he did. What was he thinking about all of this? Did he want to be married to me?

We got through the shoot with no issues and headed to a restaurant close to the hotel to celebrate and grab a bite. I decided to leave dinner early, before the celebrating could really start again. Everyone looked up as I stood. "I think I'm going to head to my room a little early tonight," I announced. "I have a bit of a headache."

"I'll walk you back," Patrick immediately volunteered, getting to his feet as well.

"What, you don't think she can cross the street by herself?" Jonah joked, but there was an underlying current of seriousness to his tone.

Patrick gave him a look but didn't respond. I thought about protesting, telling Patrick that he should stay and enjoy the party. I was sure that I could get back to the hotel on my own. Anyway, I wasn't sure that I was ready to have the conversation I knew we needed to have at the moment. I was too tired.

I didn't feel like arguing with him, though, and especially not in front of everyone. So, I let him lead me out of there.

"You doing okay?" Patrick asked worriedly as we walked.

"Yeah, just a bit hungover," I said. "I was pretty drunk last night."

"Weren't we all?" Patrick said, and from the careful way that he said it, I could tell that he was trying to figure out how much I remembered.

I decided I didn't feel like pussyfooting around it. "Were we really in a wedding chapel last night?"

Patrick was silent for a long minute. "Yeah," he finally said.

I buried my face in my hands. "Right," I said, feeling my cheeks heat up. "It was just a joke, though, right?"

Patrick cleared his throat. "Apparently not," he said weakly. "I got a call from the chapel today telling me that we can come by at any time to pick up our official marriage certificate. Apparently, our vows were the real deal."

I couldn't tell if he was happy about that fact or not. I shook my head. "We can get an annulment, though, can't we? Because it was all part of some dumb joke. Not to mention the fact that we were both drunk. Is it even legal to get married if you're both that drunk?"

"I don't know all the legalities," Patrick said, looking away from me. Had that been a flash of disappointment that I saw on his face?

Wait a second. Did Patrick *want* to be married to me?

"I'll handle it," Patrick promised me. "The annulment. Don't worry about it."

I nodded. We walked in silence back to my hotel room. For a moment there, he lingered in the doorway, looking as though he wanted to say something more. Then, he shook his head. "Good night, Emily," he said.

As he shut the door, I caught a flash of copper on his finger again. *Wait a second,* I suddenly thought. *If Patrick doesn't want to be married to me, then why the hell is he still wearing that ring?*

I leaned back against the door, unable to help feeling overwhelmed. What the hell had we done?

My phone rang, and I pulled it out and answered without thinking, even though the last thing I really wanted was to talk right now.

"Hey!" Alyssa said brightly. "Where are you at? I stopped by your parents' place and your mom said you were gone for the weekend. You're not back in the city without me, are you?"

"I'm in Niagara Falls," I admitted. "With Patrick. For a business thing."

"Ooh, how's it going?" Alyssa asked. "This is for the launch of the apparel line, right?"

I stared blankly into space for a moment. I knew that I probably shouldn't tell her, but on the other hand, I knew that I couldn't keep this to myself either. I had to talk to someone about what had happened the night before. Someone other than Patrick.

I took a deep breath. "Don't freak out, okay?" I said. "Patrick and I got married last night."

"What?" Alyssa asked, sounding shocked.

"We were both drunk, and we just went into this little chapel, and I guess we both kind of thought it was a joke, but apparently we're actually married," I blurted out.

Alyssa was silent for a long moment. Then, "Tell me everything," she demanded.

"I don't even know where to start," I sighed. But suddenly, the words came pouring out of me.

# CHAPTER 24

## PATRICK

Sitting in my lawyer's office on Monday morning couldn't have been more awkward. "You got married?" she asked. "Without a prenup? Patrick, what the hell were you thinking?" she asked.

"I don't even know," I sighed, putting my head in my hands. The weekend was like a hangover that wouldn't go away. Emily had barely looked at me on Sunday as we came home to Saratoga Springs. I had the sudden worry, as we were parting at the airport, that I would never see her again; that she would take it as an excuse to just run off back to New York.

I caught her hand, ignoring the way Jonah looked at me and then walked quickly toward the car that was waiting for us. "Emily, it's going to be okay," I told her.

She gave me a tight smile and headed for the taxi stand.

The truth was, I probably could have gotten the annulment handled in Niagara Falls. The longer I put it off, though, the longer I could tell myself that Emily was my wife.

I could tell she didn't want to be. She'd said it was

nothing more than a joke. And it was supposed to be a joke, I guess. We'd both been drunk. Only in my heart, I now realized that I had been deadly serious.

I still loved Emily. I had never stopped.

But she was insisting on an annulment, so there I was, trying to figure out what came next.

"I'm not trying to get a divorce, though," I said to my lawyer as she went on and on about divorce law in the state of New York. "We can get an annulment, can't we? Neither of us meant to actually get married. We were drunk. So it doesn't count, does it?"

I hated saying the words. They were like ash on my tongue. *It doesn't count.* For some reason, even though Emily was clearly still against us having a future together, I wanted it to count.

"In order to get an annulment," my lawyer said, sounding exasperated, "you need to both agree that you didn't mean to get married; that your judgement was impaired." She said it as though there should be some special significance to the words, but I couldn't help feeling puzzled.

"Well, it was," I said, shrugging. "We both agree that it was a mistake. Emily more so than I, even."

My lawyer sighed heavily, as though I were being particularly dense. "Patrick. Come on. You're not dumb. The Andrews family just lost all of their money, and now you think that Emily is going to let you go without trying to get anything from you?"

"She wouldn't do that," I protested. "I'm sure she's happy that I've been successful, but she wouldn't want to take that from me. Like I said, she's the one pushing for the dissolution of the marriage."

"Yes, and you don't seem too keen on letting it happen.

If you try to talk her into staying married, you could be in for a world of hurt. You're a billionaire," my lawyer said. "She doesn't have to leave you destitute to be able to live comfortably." She paused. "You said yourself that the two of you dated until she suddenly decided that you weren't rich enough for her. Now ten years later when she needs cash, suddenly she's back in your life? I'm sorry, it just seems suspicious. Could it be that she's just acting like she's pushing for the annulment because she knows you don't really want it? Then it's your idea to stay married, not hers. All she has to do is file for divorce later on and your money is hers."

I frowned. "I guess so," I said noncommittally. I couldn't picture Emily coming after me for my money. But then again, I had never expected her to break up with me for my lack of fortune either.

My lawyer shook her head. "The sooner you file, the more likely we are going to be able to protect your assets," she said. "I would suggest that you file as soon as possible."

I nodded. "All right, well, let's draw up the papers," I sighed.

"To do that, I'm going to need a copy of the marriage license," my lawyer said.

I pointed toward the paper on the desk, which Barry at the chapel had given me, stating that Emily and I were married. "I already gave you that," I reminded her.

She shook her head. "This is your marriage certificate," she said. "But before you married Emily, you would have needed to apply for a marriage license."

I shook my head. "No, we just kind of popped into the chapel as a joke. You know, to see what it would be like." My lawyer stared at me for a moment, like she could barely believe what she was hearing. "I know it was stupid," I said defensively. "We were drunk."

She shook her head, waving the words away, a grin spreading across her face. "In the state of New York, a marriage isn't legal without a marriage license. You never technically got married." She sounded relieved and triumphant.

"So I don't have to get an annulment?" I asked. "Or a divorce?"

"Nope!" she said cheerfully. "You were never actually married, so you don't need to do anything."

"Oh," I said. I knew that I should have been celebrating. Emily and I had done something pretty stupid, but at least it wasn't actually a forever kind of thing. We weren't actually married.

Instead of rejoicing, however, I couldn't help but feel disappointed. I wanted that marriage to be real. I wanted Emily to be my wife.

Even if it meant that I had to divorce her. Even if it meant that I had to give up everything to her.

Emily would be happy though, she thought that the whole thing was a mistake.

*And she's not likely to make the same mistake twice*, I realized miserably. If we weren't married now, then I knew that we would never be.

"Thanks for your help," I said to my lawyer. I was in a daze as I walked out of there. My mood continued to sour as I faced the reality of having to call Emily and explain that we had never actually been married. *She* would feel relief, I was sure.

The worst part of it all, I decided, was that I had somehow expected that things would be different between us this time. Maybe it was foolish for us to get married on a whim like that, but I had thought that somehow, we were both on the same page again.

But I had thought that once before and look how that had turned out.

I had let myself believe yet again that Emily and I might have a future. But I had just been kidding myself.

After all, we were still from two different worlds, even if now I was the one with money and her the one without. How could I ever have thought that things might work out?

# CHAPTER 25

## EMILY

I tried to clean up my desk on Thursday afternoon before I headed home for the night. Or, to my parents' new condo, anyway. The place still didn't feel like home, but it was starting to feel marginally better now that my parents were settling in some. Mom was still upset, and Dad was still feeling terribly guilty about the whole thing, but they were both starting to seem alive again, and that was what counted.

I hadn't been sure if I would still have a job come Monday morning, not least because of the whole chapel debacle. I had figured that if nothing else, I needed to go in there and gather my belongings. Patrick had come into my office first thing in the morning with a whole new stack of designs. "I know it's a little preemptive since we don't even know if this line is going to take off, but I was hoping we could start on the next round of ideas. Ideally, if the line does well, this would launch right after Thanksgiving to give people some new things to buy heading into the holidays and winter sport season."

"Sure thing," I told him. The designs were even more

primitive than his first ones, having not been developed at all yet, so it was a whole new time-consuming project for me and the team to work on. In addition to that, we were still working on some marketing concepts for the line that was launching now.

I gathered up some of the photos from the Niagara Falls shoot, smiling down at them. Whatever else had happened on that trip, the photos had turned out phenomenal. I could still barely believe my work was going to be showcased.

Patrick would be sending them out soon in anticipation of the full launch of his line. The designs had already been sent to the manufacturers. I knew the line was going to be a huge hit. I just wished I could feel excited.

Instead, I just felt miserable. It was all I could do that week to throw myself into my work and try to forget all about Patrick and me. Since we'd returned, Patrick had barely said two words to me, even in regard to work. He was keeping his distance.

I had ruined whatever friendship we had managed to rebuild, and I hated that.

On the other hand, what was I supposed to do, stay married to him? I couldn't do that. It wouldn't have been right. Hell, I barely remembered *getting* married to him. None of it was the way that it should have been.

The worst part was that the more Patrick avoided me around the office, the more I seemed incapable of thinking of anything other than him. I would find my focus drifting during meetings as I wondered what he was up to. Every day as I ate my lunch alone, I wished that he were sitting there across from me, cracking jokes and getting me out of my miserable head state.

I wished he would at least tell me the status of our

annulment. Was there anything that I needed to sign? Were we still married?

I didn't want to ask him about it because of how awkward the situation was.

The trouble was, I couldn't tell him the real reason that I couldn't start a relationship with him now.

I was too scared. It was that simple. He had everything figured out and my life was just one shitshow after another. I'd always thought I was so superior, but the mighty had definitely fallen. I hadn't even managed to finish my degree yet. He had managed to build a successful business from the ground up, a business that he was currently in the process of expanding. He was sexy as all hell, and he was a billionaire. I felt like a failure next to him.

What could I bring to our relationship, really? Before, all I'd had was Daddy's money. I wanted to make something of myself before I committed to Patrick. I wanted to have something of my own to bring to the table.

Now I was realizing that I would never be able to bring as much to the table as Patrick did. I didn't feel like I deserved him.

So, we needed to get that annulment so he could move on and find someone worthy of him. But how did I ask about it without hurting him again?

When I really thought about it, I *wanted* to stay married to him. I wanted to build a life with him. Not because of his money or his good looks or any of that. Because he was Patrick. The guy that I had been in love with for my whole life, I only now realized.

What would it be like to wake up with him every morning? Would we have kids one day? Would I keep my job here as a designer, or would I be able to launch my own line of clothing? Where would we live? There were so many questions, and as I lay in bed each night, I found myself imagining different scenarios.

I always woke up the next morning feeling miserable again, though. Those were just dreams, nothing more. They would never come true.

When I got back to the condo that evening, I found an envelope that had been pushed under the door. I frowned and picked it up. It was addressed to me. I shut the door behind me and slit it open, wondering what it could be.

My jaw dropped when I saw the letter, scrawled in red ink. *Leave Patrick Manning alone, bitch.*

It was such a juvenile, stupid threat, but I felt fear immediately spill through me. I sank down to the floor, the letter dropping into my lap.

Who could have written the letter? Who knew where my parents' new condo was? But of course, the whole town knew that, by this point. We'd had plenty of neighbors drop by already to wish my parents well, bringing them housewarming gifts, and pretend they weren't gloating over our financial downfall. That didn't narrow it down.

Who knew about Patrick and me? The trouble was, that could be anyone as well. It was no secret, really, that we had dated in high school. And it was no secret now that I was working for his company. This wasn't a very big town, there was no keeping secrets.

I swallowed hard. There were plenty of people who might have wanted to warn me away from Patrick. Starting with people in the company, if they had found out about us, and ending with some sort of crazy stalker who wanted Patrick for herself. He was a billionaire, and a very attractive one at that. In fact, when his magazine spread was finally published last week, with him in that jockey uniform, he'd been the talk of the office. Faith, his secretary, said that he had gotten a deluge of messages asking for dates, and even a few crazy women offering to have his babies for money.

Could one of those people also be keeping tabs on the people that Patrick was close to?

I wasn't sure what to do. If I went to the police, I was sure that I would have to answer more awkward questions than it was worth. I wasn't even sure how to answer some of the questions. What was my relationship to Patrick?

Not only would that lead to awkward questions from the authorities, but it would also mean spilling the beans in a small town. No one knew that Patrick and I had slept together again. No one knew about the wedding. Jonah might suspect something, but I didn't think that even he *knew*.

I couldn't spill those secrets. It could cause a scandal for Patrick that could impact his company.

I would just have to make sure to keep our relationship strictly professional. The annulment would come through soon, if it hadn't already, and then maybe all of this would just go away.

# CHAPTER 26

## PATRICK

It had been over a week since I had found out that Emily and I were never technically married, and I still hadn't told her. I didn't know why I was putting it off. In some way, I knew that it wasn't fair to keep pretending like we were actually married. I just didn't know what to say to her, and I didn't want to see the look of relief on her face when she found out that the marriage had never actually been valid.

We'd been busy at work; that was the excuse that I tried to give myself. Between the launch of the new line and getting started on the follow-up products that we hoped to launch, there was plenty to do. I hoped that she was just distracted and not thinking about it.

Of course, that was stupid. I couldn't get the marriage off my mind, and I was the one who knew that it was all a sham from the start. I kept thinking about what it would have been like if it wasn't. Maybe we hadn't planned to get married, but what if we actually had and had decided that, instead of an annulment, we'd try to make the best of things?

Didn't our history sort of show that we were meant to be together, anyway?

Except that when I really thought about it, our history was nothing more than me building up our relationship in my head until it all came tumbling back down.

I'd been avoiding Emily as much as I could around work, knowing that it was for the best. If I didn't see her, then she couldn't ask me about the status of our marriage, and if I didn't see her, then I couldn't make things worse.

Of course, if I didn't see her, that in itself was its own form of punishment, because I wanted nothing more than to be around her, to enjoy her smile and her laughter, to be *with* her. Even if I knew now that I could never have her, at least I could let myself pretend for a little while longer.

Seeing her was a unique form of torture. Our wedding night, fake though it may have been, was one of the best nights of my life. I didn't think that I had ever felt that content before, not even back when we were in high school and I thought that everything was sure to work out between us.

The trouble was, now I knew that I would probably never get another night like that. Not even for fun. I had well and truly fucked things up this time. Even though I wasn't ready to let her go, I knew that she would never want me again. I would never get to hold her again.

When we were younger, it had felt like we would have all the time in the world. Now, the timing had just never been right, and I kept acting on my basest impulses.

I sighed and looked out the window of my office. I should probably get some lunch soon, but I didn't have much of an appetite, and had felt generally miserable, since we'd gotten back from Niagara Falls.

There was a knock on my door. I turned and was surprised to see Emily standing there. She raised an eyebrow at me. "Alright, I was waiting for you to come to me, but you know I'm not that patient," she said, putting her hands on her hips. "Any chance you've resolved our little problem yet? Is there anything that I need to sign?"

I swallowed hard. "I have some news, actually," I admitted. God, she was going to hate me even more when she found out how long I'd been sitting on this. I should have told her a week ago that we had never officially been married, as far as the state of New York was concerned.

Why had I held off? Because I liked the dream of it. Telling her that we were never married at all just made it seem so final. Like we didn't have any sort of future, like there was nothing tying us together at all.

I had quit wearing the ring that she had bought me in the chapel gift shop, but only because it had turned my finger green. It was still there in the top drawer of my desk, and every time I opened it to grab a pen, I thought of her.

Now was the time to tell her. I couldn't hold off for any longer.

"Can we go to lunch?" Emily asked, much to my surprise. "We can talk about it there." She glanced back over her shoulder, like she was expecting to see someone there. Like she thought I might have told the whole office about our shenanigans.

I frowned but nodded. "Sure. Why don't we head down to the café on the ground floor?"

Emily shook her head. "You know where Little Nick's is? Can we meet there in about twenty minutes?"

I blinked. Little Nick's did great sandwiches, and I went there every once in a while for lunch. That in itself wasn't out of the ordinary. But why were we meeting there instead of going over together?

"We could walk over now," I pointed out slowly.

Emily shook her head again. "I have a couple other errands I need to do in town. Picking up some dry-cleaning. You know, the prototypes that we sent in to be cleaned after the photoshoot. So I was thinking I would grab them on the way. I don't want to bore you. I'll just meet you there."

She was stammering and sounded uncertain, and I knew there was more to the story than that. Whatever it was, though, things were complicated enough between the two of us that I didn't really want to press her.

"Okay," I said. "See you there."

When I got to the restaurant, Emily wasn't there yet, but I wasn't worried. She had errands to do, after all. She finally arrived, empty-handed.

I frowned at her. "Where's the dry-cleaning?"

She looked puzzled for a second and then blushed slightly. "Sorry, that was kind of an excuse," she said. What was going on with her?

We took a table near the back and ordered our food. "So how is the annulment process coming along?" Emily whispered.

I frowned at her again. "Why are you whispering?" I asked. There was no one within earshot. The restaurant was practically empty.

Emily pursed her lips. "Quit dodging the question," she said. "It's been over a week and you haven't said anything about it. What's going on?"

I stared at her for a moment. I wanted to ask what was going on with her. I understood that she didn't want to be married to me, and that she was probably worried that someone would find out. But this level of caution seemed excessive.

I knew that if I said anything, though, she would just accuse me of dodging again.

This was it. The time was here. I had to come clean. I took a deep breath.

# CHAPTER 27

## EMILY

It felt like a risk seeing Patrick in public like this, but it felt like more of a risk to discuss the annulment in the office. Eventually, I had decided that this was the better option. I knew that I was confusing him with my attempts at ultra-secrecy, but I wouldn't have to explain that if he would just tell me that the annulment was finalized. If there was nothing more tying the two of us together, then whoever was stalking him would have nothing more to say to me.

We would both be safe. That was all I wanted, for Patrick to be safe.

"I saw my lawyer," Patrick finally said. "Apparently in order for a marriage to be legally binding in the state of New York, we would've had to apply for a marriage license first. Just the ceremony isn't good enough."

I sat back in shock, my eyes widening. Was he saying what I thought he was saying? That we weren't actually married? That I had been waiting all this time for an annulment, only to find out that we never needed one in the first place?

"Are you absolutely sure that we didn't pay for a marriage license somehow that night?" I asked carefully.

"We didn't," Patrick confirmed. "I called Barry to double check. They can't grant marriage licenses there." He paused, grimacing. "I think they may have realized that we probably shouldn't actually be getting married, and that's why they let us just go through with it. You remember Barry's whole thing about the divorce rate."

"Actually, I don't," I told him flatly. "I barely remember anything about being there."

Patrick looked down at his hands, and I could see that he felt ashamed. I felt sort of bad for that. He hadn't done a terrible thing, really. Especially not since I knew that he had been nearly as drunk as I was.

I was starting to wonder if it was ever going to be the right time or place for 'us.' I doubted it.

"Why did you take so long to tell me that we weren't actually married?" I asked him quietly.

Patrick grimaced and shrugged. "Was it really so bad being secretly married to a billionaire for a little while?" he asked.

"Except that we were never married," I reminded him coolly. He didn't answer. I didn't know what to say. "If we were married, I'd hate to start out with lies."

He flinched as though I had hit him. "I guess it doesn't matter," he finally said, "because you and I are never actually going to be married."

The food came out just then. I didn't really have an appetite, but I was the one who had invited him to lunch. Besides, I had already confused him enough today. What if he started asking questions?

I didn't want to tell him about the note I'd gotten. I wasn't sure why. Was I afraid that he would care too little about my safety if he knew about it? Or was I more worried that he would care too much and that it would leave me wanting more?

I forced myself to eat as though everything was normal. It had to be someone from work, that much I was sure of. They were the only ones who had really seen Patrick and me together. That was the reason I'd been avoiding him around the office, and the reason why I'd wanted to come here for lunch. As long as we were careful, things would be fine now.

I just wanted more than fine. That was the problem.

I stood abruptly. "I'm going to get a box for the rest of my food so that I can head back to work," I said. "I always forget how big the full sandwiches are here. I should have just ordered a half."

Patrick stared up at me, slowly chewing a bite of his food. He wiped his mouth with a napkin and started to say something, but I cut him off before he could. "Don't worry about walking me back to work. I can get there on my own."

"Emily," Patrick said, and I could hear a quiet note of sad desperation in his tone.

I shook my head. "Don't, Patrick. Give me some time."

He finally nodded, staring down at his plate. I decided not to bother waiting for a box and instead just headed back to the office.

Once there, I sighed and slumped back against the back wall of the elevator. That couldn't have gone worse, really. Not only did I have to give up on the delusion that we had ever been married, but I was pretty sure that now I had to give up on the delusion that we were even still friends. That hurt more than I'd expected it to. I felt tears prick the corners of my eyes, and I furiously brushed them away.

Just in time, too. The elevator chimed, and Faith got on. She raised an eyebrow at me. "Where's Patrick?" she asked.

"I don't know," I immediately said, my heart beating a little faster.

Faith frowned. "He told me the two of you were having lunch together."

I winced internally. "We were. We did," I said. "But I finished early, and I have a ton of things that I need to do this afternoon. I'm sure he'll be back soon if you need him."

Faith looked like she wanted to ask more questions, but thankfully, we reached my floor just then. I darted past her. "Got to go!" I chirped. The doors closed behind me, and I took a deep breath. Was it possible that Faith was the crazy stalker?

It could be, I decided. I knew that she was close to Patrick and that she was more than a little suspicious of me in the beginning. They had worked together for a long time now. Maybe she had feelings for him that went beyond the professional. She also knew the man's schedule and every appointment that he made with me. Plus, she knew about the trip to Niagara Falls.

I had to keep an eye on her, I decided. She definitely could be the stalker.

# CHAPTER 28

## PATRICK

I couldn't help feeling distracted during my meeting with Jonah on Thursday. I had passed Emily in the hallway that morning, and she had barely made eye contact with me. I missed her. We hadn't talked at all since our lunch on Monday, and she was acting so weird then.

I wanted to make sure that she was okay. I had screwed things up; that much was obvious from the way that she practically ran out of the restaurant to get away from me. It seemed like something more than just the marriage debacle, though.

Unless it was that other thing she said in the restaurant, about how if we were actually married, she would hope that we didn't start off with lies. I could kick myself for the response that I had given her, too; *I guess it doesn't matter, because you and I are never actually going to be married.*

I knew the minute that the words were out of my mouth that I had to find some way to take them back. Granted, they were the truth. Emily had made it pretty damn clear that she considered being married to me the worst scenario possible. All the same, when I said it like that, with so much finality, I could see the pain streak across her face.

Like in another time and place, she would have wished for a different future for us.

Where had it all gone wrong? I wished I knew. I wished I could just talk to her about it. Let her know how I really felt. I doubted that would make things better, though.

I wasn't sure that there *was* any way to make things better between us. As much as that killed me, maybe it was time to let Emily go.

But I couldn't seem to do that. I wanted her as my wife for real. Even though we weren't even dating. I wanted to figure out how I had somehow managed to fuck everything up again.

Suddenly, Jonah sighed. "Patrick are you even listening to me?" he asked.

I jolted, looking guiltily over at him. I realized that I didn't have a single idea what he had just been saying. And what's worse, this wasn't the first time that he had called me out during this meeting.

"Sorry," I sighed. "It's nothing."

"It's Emily, isn't it?"

I scowled at him. "I told you, there's nothing between us," I said defensively.

"Oh, bullshit," Jonah said. "I could see the sparks flying in Niagara Falls. What happened after I left the bar that night?"

I stared at him for a long moment and then sighed, putting my head in my hands. "You wouldn't believe me if I told you," I said flatly.

"Try me," Jonah retorted evenly.

I frowned, but I was sick of trying to hide it from everyone. Especially from Jonah. I was closer to him than anyone else. I had to tell him about it, even if only to get it out of my own head a bit.

"Emily and I dated in high school," I began. "We were high school sweethearts. I thought we were really going to make it work, but the night that we graduated, she basically told me that she didn't want to be with me and that she was going off to Europe the next year by herself."

"Ouch," Jonah said.

"When I saw her back here, well, I didn't think of it as a second chance," I continued. "She made it pretty clear that she wasn't interested in that. But I couldn't seem to keep my hands off her." I took a deep breath. "And then when we went to Niagara Falls, we both got drunk that night and went for a walk and we found a wedding chapel."

Jonah groaned. "You didn't," he said.

"It was just supposed to be a joke." I shrugged. "I guess the joke's on me, because it *was* just a joke in the end. Since we just had the ceremony but no license, we were never actually married."

"But you thought that you were?" Jonah asked. "More importantly, she thought that you were?"

"Until yesterday," I confirmed. "I mean, I knew that it was a sham since early last week. I talked to my lawyer about getting an annulment, and she cleared things up."

Jonah frowned, his brow furrowing. "Wait, so you let her believe that you were married for a week and a half?" he asked.

"I should have told her sooner," I sighed. "I just didn't want to face the fact that it was over between us. She never wanted to be married to me in the first place."

Jonah frowned. "Have you ever thought that maybe she just didn't want to drunkenly marry you in some kitschy chapel with no prior planning?" he asked. "Did you even have a ring for her or anything?"

"No," I sighed. I shook my head. "Either way, it doesn't matter. She's barely talking to me at this point."

"So what are you going to do?" Jonah asked, to my surprise. "I mean, I've never seen you like this about anyone before. You really care about her, don't you?"

"I'm in love with her; I always have been," I admitted. "But Emily has never arranged her life according to my feelings. Anyway, you should have seen how quick she was to remind me that it was just supposed to be a joke."

Jonah shook his head. "Maybe after all these years, she just wanted the timing and place to be right," he said. "Maybe she wanted you to, I don't know, treat her well. Have you guys even been on a date since high school?"

I ducked my head. "No," I told him. I sighed. "I'm her boss. I can't really date her anyway."

Jonah made a face. "Look, I feel like I should be reminding you that if this doesn't work out, you're probably going to lose a great employee. But I can already tell that if this doesn't work out, you're not going to be able to focus on or celebrate the success of anything that we're working toward here. So why not give it another go?"

"How?" I asked him. "She's barely speaking to me, remember? Hell, she barely looks at me."

"Sweep her off her feet," Jonah said. "Woo her. Bring on the romance. Do it up big." He paused. "You must have figured out something she liked before. You got her to go out with you in high school."

I considered his words.

I thought about the flowers that I had put in her locker in high school. Every single day for a week, I'd put a new one in there, just hoping to get her attention. I had been persistent, even when it seemed like she wanted nothing to do with me.

Really, the situation wasn't all that different now.

In any case, it was worth a try. I was starting to realize just how impossible it would be for me to keep living without her.

# CHAPTER 29

## EMILY

On Wednesday, there was another mystery package on my desk when I arrived at work. I sighed when I saw it.

Monday, it had been a huge bouquet of at least fifty sunflowers and no card. They made me want to cry just looking at them, but I refused to go running to Patrick to ask what the meaning of it was.

I couldn't get his words out of my mind from lunch. I knew that I shouldn't have said that thing about lies, but did he really have to make it sound like he would never have wanted to marry me? Ever?

But then why had he waited a week and a half to tell me that the marriage wasn't even legal? If the thought of being tied to me was so awful, why hadn't he said so outright?

Now, he had started out the week sending me bouquets of sunflowers. Then on Tuesday, there had been chocolates shaped like sunflowers. Today, I opened the box to find a dozen carefully crafted cupcakes with frosting sunflowers on top. Once again, there was no card, but it didn't take a genius to figure out who was sending these things.

It made me nervous receiving all of them there in the office. What if the stalker was there and managed to put two and two together? Hell, what if Patrick was dictating his orders to Faith and she really *was* the stalker?

I had yet to receive another threatening note, and it wasn't exactly my fault that I was receiving all of the gifts. I was doing my absolute best to stay away from Patrick. What was I supposed to do, march up there and tell him to quit sending me things?

I had a sneaking suspicion that I knew how that one would go. Somehow, we would go from yelling at one another to fucking in his office or something like that.

I lifted one of the cupcakes out of the box. Well, if he was going to send me cupcakes, I might as well eat them. I had to admit, they looked pretty good. Patrick was going all out this time.

It made me wonder if he really did want me. It made me wonder, for just a second, what it would be like to have Patrick court me for real. I knew that he was a romantic at heart. He always had been. What would it be like to have his full adult charm turned on me?

The idea of that scared me a little bit. It was overwhelming to think about. But for the first time, it scared me in a good way. It made pleasure shoot through me. I wondered why I had always been so worried about us building a future together.

Somehow, in knowing that he had lied to me about the annulment, I realized just how much I trusted him. I didn't think he had ever lied to me about anything else. And that meant that when he told me that he loved me, he really meant it.

Of course, it had been a long time since he had said anything like that. As my eyes slipped back toward the cupcakes, though, I realized that he had been saying it without words ever since I had come back into his life. Hell, he had been the one to hatch a plan to get married. We might have been drunk at the time, and it might have felt like a joke, but there was something real there too. I was sure of it.

I bit into the cupcake. It was chocolate, and it was every bit as amazing as I'd expected it to be. It was decadent and delicious and everything that I needed in my life to cope with my heartache just then. As I was halfway through it, though, a sudden wave of nausea hit me, and the next thing I knew, I was running for the bathroom. I threw up the second the stall door closed behind me.

Afterwards, I frowned, kneeling there on the tile. Must have been something that I ate for lunch. Although come to think of it, I had been feeling a little flu-like that week; tired, and like my temperature was all out of whack. Maybe I was actually getting sick.

Hopefully it could wait until the weekend. I had tons of other stuff that I needed to get done, with the launch of the new apparel line coming up quickly.

I put all thoughts of sickness out of my mind. *If I don't think too hard about it, then I won't get sick*, I stubbornly told myself. Although that didn't seem to be the case, I didn't feel like I was getting any worse, and that at least was a relief.

The gifts continued all week, and by Friday afternoon, it felt like my entire office was full of sunflowers or things that looked like sunflowers. Alyssa's eyes widened when she came in. "Whoa," she said. "What's all this?"

"What are you doing here?" I asked in surprise.

"I was hoping we could go to lunch today." She raised an eyebrow at me. "You've been basically incommunicado since, you know, Niagara Falls. I just wanted to make sure that you're okay."

"I'm fine," I sighed. I gestured around the office. "Actually, this is all from a secret admirer, apparently. But I'm sure it's from Patrick. It's been like this ever since he told me that we're not actually married."

Alyssa frowned. "Why would he send you a bunch of sunflowers if you're not married?" she asked.

I shrugged. "No clue. Haven't talked to him about it," I said. "But this is pretty much exactly the same move that he pulled when we were in school to get me to go out with him. I think he just wants my attention."

Alyssa shook her head. Was that a hint of jealousy in her eyes? Before I could dwell on that for too much longer, I was hit with another of those nasty waves of nausea. I ran to the bathroom and threw up again, for what felt like the billionth time that week.

When I came out of the stall, my friend was there waiting for me. "So, I take it you probably don't want to go to lunch, huh?" she asked. "Are you all right?"

"Yeah," I sighed. "Just the flu or something. I think a couple people have it. I've been throwing up pretty much every afternoon. But I typically feel fine afterward."

Alyssa's eyebrows rose in surprise. "That doesn't sound much like the flu to me," she said, tapping her long nails against her arm. "How long has this been going on?"

"I don't know," I sighed. "It's been pretty much every day this week."

"Are you sure you're not pregnant?"

I stared at her for a moment, then grabbed at the sink, my legs feeling like jelly. Was it possible? Could my nausea really be morning sickness? The rest of the symptoms I'd been feeling would line up as well. Exhaustion, headaches...

I'd been telling myself that I was just pushing myself too hard with the new launch and work on the next product line. But maybe Alyssa was right.

I thought back to when my last period had been, but I could barely remember. With all the drama from my parents and work and moving, I had definitely missed one, which wasn't all too surprising except that normally my periods came like clockwork, no matter how much travel and chaos was in my life at the time.

Alyssa was still staring at me, not seeming to know what to say. "Why don't I run to the drugstore on the corner and grab a pregnancy test?" she finally suggested.

I nodded faintly. I was still waiting in the bathroom when she came back.

"All right, I think you should use this right now," Alyssa said, herding me into a stall and handing me the package.

I suddenly shook my head. "I'm at work," I reminded her. "The last thing I need is for the janitor or someone to find this." Or worse.

After all, my boss was the one whose baby it would be if I was pregnant. I shuddered at the thought.

Alyssa rolled her eyes. "Come on, we both know you're not going to be able to stop worrying about it now," she said. "No one will know that it's yours. Just take it and get it over with, then put it in the tampon bag. No one's going to dig through there to find it."

I sighed, but I knew she was right. I wasn't going to be able to do anything for the rest of the day if I didn't find this out.

I locked the stall door and read the instructions. The minutes ticked by, and eventually I had my answer.

I stared down at the stick in my hand.

Pregnant.

# CHAPTER 30

## PATRICK

I was dying to know what Emily thought of all the sunflower gifts, but I hadn't heard a single word out of her. I couldn't help feeling frustrated and annoyed. I knew that I shouldn't. If she didn't want anything to do with me, then she didn't want anything to do with me. Still, I would have at least thought she would tell me that she wanted me to stop.

Instead, I hadn't heard anything.

I finally went to her office on Monday morning. I couldn't stand waiting anymore.

I knocked on the door and then poked my head in to see if she was there. When I saw that she was, I stepped inside, closing and locking the door behind myself. "We need to talk," I told her firmly. I just needed to know where we stood. It was going to be impossible to keep working with her otherwise.

I froze as I stepped closer to Emily. She was sitting behind her desk looking pale, dark circles beneath her eyes. "Are you okay?" I asked slowly, concern filling me.

"I'm fine," Emily said. "Just a little tired. That's all."

I frowned. "I hate to say it, but you look more than a little tired." I paused. "I know things have been busy with the launch of the new line. I probably should have waited before handing you the next set of designs, I was just so excited with the way the last ones came together."

"It's fine, really. I'm fine," Emily said.

I cleared my throat. "I know that things between us have been off as well..." I trailed off, not sure what to say. It wasn't fair for me to assume that she wasn't sleeping much just because I was having a hard time sleeping at night, plagued by thoughts of her.

Emily shook her head sharply. "That's not it," she said. "Really, Patrick, I'm fine. I'm just a little tired. But it's nothing that I can't manage."

I stared at her for a long moment. I wasn't buying it. I pulled out my phone and called Faith. "I just wanted to let you know that I'll be taking the rest of the day off. I want to take Emily home; she's not feeling well."

"Patrick, no. Come on," Emily protested. "You're making a ridiculous fuss."

I shook my head at her and finished up my phone call with my secretary. "Come on," I said. "Let's get your things." I helped her gather them up and then herded her out of the office.

The whole way home, Emily continued to insist that she was fine, but the more she said it, the less I believed it. I parked out in front of her family's new condo. "Is anyone home?" I asked her.

"I don't know," Emily sighed, sounding peevish. "You going to come up and see?"

"As a matter of fact, yeah," I said, wondering just what the heck was going on with her. I knew that we had had our problems lately, but I had never heard her be so snappish before. I remembered how weird she had been when I told her that we were never really married in the first place, and I wondered if this somehow stemmed back to that.

I couldn't help but feel worried for her. She looked awful.

We went upstairs. There was no one in the condo. "You don't have to stay," Emily said as I toed off my shoes.

"Why don't you go lie down on the couch?" I suggested, turning her toward the living room. As we walked in, I saw that my sunflower gifts had found a home here. At least she was keeping them, even if she still hadn't said anything about them.

Emily laid down on the couch, and I covered her with a blanket. Then I headed into the kitchen and nosed around until I could find something to put together for lunch.

"What are you doing?" Emily called from the living room.

I brought her a glass of water and set it on the coffee table. "Heating up some soup for lunch and making grilled cheese."

Emily sighed. "I'm not hungry, Pat," she complained grumpily.

"I want you to at least try to take a few bites," I said. "Come on, Emily. I'm worried about you. You don't look like you feel very good."

She huffed, but that seemed to have done the trick. I went back into the kitchen to continue making the food. When I came back out and set the bowl and plate down on the coffee table, Emily took a few small bites.

I sat on the armchair across from her, watching approvingly. "So, I see you've been getting my gifts," I couldn't resist saying.

Emily gave me a small smile. "I knew it was you sending

them." She paused, taking another small sip of her tomato soup. "They're really lovely, but you need to stop. You know that."

I grimaced and looked down. "Why?" I asked.

"You're my boss," she reminded me. "We said we were going to keep things professional, remember?"

"I think that ship has sailed." I paused. "To be honest, I don't want to keep things strictly professional anymore." Emily looked up in surprise, but I refused to back down. I knew I was about to cross another line, but I couldn't hold back. "I realized the night of our fake wedding that I can't keep away from you, and I don't want to try to anymore. I want you. I want you to give me a chance."

Emily stared at me, her eyes wide, and I knew that I had gone too far. But it was too late to take any of it back, even if I'd wanted to.

# CHAPTER 31

## EMILY

I stared at Patrick, trying to think of something to say. He wanted me. He had said that he couldn't stay away. It didn't sound like he was saying that he never wanted to marry me. Hope soared inside of me. Was it possible that Patrick somehow still loved me, after everything that we had been through?

It was what I had been hoping for all last week, with the gifts that he kept sending me. I kept hoping that it meant that he was thinking about the first time that he had asked me out, back in high school. That he was remembering the future that he had planned for us back then.

That maybe we could have that future now.

The thought of it scared me. But with a baby growing inside of me—*his* baby—I realized that I wanted nothing more than to have Patrick by my side for the rest of my life. To raise a family with him. Not just because he was a huge romantic. I wanted him because he was the same guy that I fell in love with all those years ago; honest, smart, caring, and fun.

The trouble was, there were just too many complications.

First of all, he was my boss. I didn't want to give up my job with his company, but I also knew just how terribly things could go wrong with the two of us. I didn't want to ruin my design reputation that way or ruin his reputation right as he was starting a new business venture.

Especially since there was still the matter of whoever wrote that threatening note telling me to stay away from him. What if that person became angrier? What if they tried to hurt me, or Patrick, or the baby? I couldn't stand to think that something might happen to one of us.

Besides, we still had never talked about graduation night, or the fact that the tables were now turned, or really anything of substance regarding a relationship. It had all been so impulsive this time around. We had sex because we couldn't keep our hands off one another. You couldn't build a relationship on that.

Above all else, I knew that we couldn't start a relationship on lies. At the moment, though, I just couldn't bring myself to tell him about the baby. He was being so nice to me right now, taking care of me. He thought I was sick or had the flu or something. He didn't know what was actually wrong.

I should tell him that I was pregnant. We couldn't start a relationship until I did so. But how could I possibly tell him? I had no idea if he even wanted children at this stage in his life. We were still so new to one another again and having a baby together was like pushing fast forward on the whole thing.

"I don't think dating is a good idea right now," I heard myself say.

"Why not?" Patrick asked, and I could tell from his tone

that he was ready to argue with any excuse that I could come up with. I loved him a little more for that.

Before I could say anything, I was hit with my daily dose of nausea and had to run to the bathroom to throw up. Afterwards, I lay there on the tile floor, pressing my forehead against the cool tiles on the wall. How was I going to face Patrick now? Would he suspect the real cause? It hadn't taken Alyssa long to figure out what was actually happening.

I felt a thrum of worry pulse through me, but when Patrick came to find me, he was unbelievably gentle, scooping me up in his arms. "I can walk," I protested weakly, even as I snuggled closer to him. It felt good to rest my cheek against his chest. As though everything was somehow going to be all right.

"Where's your room?" Patrick asked.

"The one on the left," I said, and he carried me straight to my bed. He then lay down beside me, curling his body around mine and holding me close. I knew that I couldn't possibly have the relationship that I wanted with him, or the one that he seemed to want, but for now, I was too tired to argue with him. It was comforting to have him there with me, anyway. I couldn't make him leave.

He stayed well into the evening, even though I insisted, after a nap, that I was feeling much better. When he finally left, he kissed me on the forehead. "I'll see you soon, okay?" he said. "Don't worry about coming into work tomorrow if you still feel crummy, either."

I nodded. "Thanks, Pat," I said quietly.

"Call me if you need anything," he said, smiling gently at me. He headed toward the door, pausing with his hand on the knob. "By the way, I hope you don't think I'm going to stop wooing you just because you don't think now is the right time to date. I'm not taking no for an answer."

I laughed. "I'd expect nothing different," I said, a happy smile on my face for the first time in days. I couldn't help feeling overjoyed at the way that he cared for me.

Maybe it was time to throw caution to the wind and give my heart what it wanted. Patrick should be able to keep me safe, shouldn't he? Besides, I hadn't received any more threats after that first one. Maybe there was nothing to really be worried about.

I dozed in and out for a little while, imagining the family that Patrick and I could have together. He and I, plus our little one. I liked the idea of that.

A little while later, my phone rang. I picked it up without even checking to see who it was. "Hello?" I asked groggily.

A mechanical voice on the other end let me know that it was the stalker. "You've crossed a line," they said. "Give him up or there will be hell to pay."

I immediately hung up, my hands shaking so badly that I dropped the phone. I curled up tightly in the blankets for a moment, tears pricking the corners of my eyes. I wanted to call Patrick, to ask him to rush back over here and protect me. I knew I couldn't do that, though.

The police. Maybe it was time to get the authorities involved.

I picked up my phone and opened the call log, but all I could see was that the previous number was listed as 'unknown.'

It had to be Faith, though, didn't it? Patrick had immediately called his secretary and told him that he was taking the afternoon off because I was sick. Shit, I should have realized what a terrible problem that was. I should have said something.

She was the only person who had known that Patrick was here. It had to be her.

I swallowed hard. Next time I was in the office, I was going to have to talk to her.

# CHAPTER 32

## PATRICK

I was shocked to see Faith tumble into my office on Tuesday afternoon. She was visibly upset, and I was immediately alarmed. "What's wrong?" I asked. "Faith, are you okay?"

She shook her head, sniffling. "Emily just cornered me and accused me of making threats against her," she wailed.

"What?" I asked, even more shocked now. Surely, I hadn't heard that right.

"Apparently someone is stalking her or something and threatening to hurt her if she doesn't stay away from you," Faith said. "I don't know, you should talk to her about it. I just didn't want you to think that I might do something like that. I swear it's not me. I have no idea what she's talking about."

I shook my head. "No, I know you wouldn't do something like that." Of course she wouldn't. Faith was one of my longest-standing employees with the company. She'd been with me from the very start. I trusted her with pretty much everything. And in response, she looked out for me as though we were family.

I couldn't believe what Emily had accused her of, but at the same time, my fears for Emily overwhelmed nearly every other rational thought. Had Faith just said that Emily had been receiving threats?

"Faith, why don't you go home for the afternoon?" I suggested, my voice sounding strangled even to my own ears. "I'll talk to Emily." I didn't wait to hear her response as I practically bolted for the next floor down.

I burst into Emily's office without knocking, startling the team of designers that were gathered in there with her. I forced a tight smile on my face. "Hey guys, would you mind giving us a second?" I asked them.

They looked confused, but they dutifully scurried off to their own desks. I shut the door behind them. "Faith says you just told her you were being stalked," I said immediately.

Emily let out a breath and nodded, reaching into her bag and pulling out a piece of paper. It was a note warning her to stay away from me. "They've been calling me as well," she said, and I could hear how upset she was.

"Why didn't you tell me?" I couldn't resist asking.

Emily only shrugged and looked unhappily away from me. "It has to be Faith," she said unhappily. "She's the only one who knows when you're spending time with me."

I shook my head sharply. "Faith wouldn't do this," I said. "She's protective of me, but she's not a psycho." I sighed. "You should have told me about this sooner, before you accused her of threatening you." I paused. "You should move into my place so I can keep an eye on you."

Emily's jaw dropped. "I can't do that," she finally managed to say. "Patrick, wouldn't that just make the stalker angrier?"

"I'm going to keep you safe," I promised her.

"How?" she asked. "Patrick, I know you're, like, an athletic god, but we don't even know who's threatening me or why."

"I don't care," I said. "I'm going to keep you safe. I don't want you alone in your parents' place. I need you where I can see you. Please."

Those final words might have come out a little too raw with emotion. Emily's eyes widened. But finally, she nodded. "Okay," she said quietly.

# CHAPTER 33

## EMILY

I listened as Patrick talked on the phone with Jonah. I couldn't seem to concentrate on anything else, so I just sat at my desk, staring down at my hands, while I listened to him plot my foreseeable future. Right now, they were talking about security firms.

I felt tears prick the corners of my eyes. Stupid hormones. Everything was upsetting at the moment, and only getting more so.

As I listened to Patrick talk, it was like he had suddenly stepped in and taken control of my life, like I didn't even have a say in things anymore. Before I realized it, he was escorting me back to his own office, where Jonah was making the arrangements for a security team to deal with potential threats against me.

"I don't want a security team following me everywhere," I protested weakly.

"And I don't want to see anything bad happen to you," Patrick all but growled.

Wasn't this what I had been afraid of in the first place?

Patrick having this idea of how our lives should be and imposing that iron will on me? I didn't want this.

But I was helpless to stop it now, the wheels were already in motion.

"Now who's the one who's acting crazy?" I muttered under my breath. Fortunately, neither Patrick nor Jonah appeared to have heard me.

The team arrived in record speed. "All right, next stop, we're going to your place to pack your things," Patrick informed me. He turned to his business partner. "Jonah, I'm sorry, but I'm going to be out for the rest of the day. Can you handle this afternoon's meeting?"

"Don't worry about it," Jonah said. "I think it's understandable, in light of the circumstances."

"There are no circumstances," I snapped, folding my arms across my chest. "And Patrick, for the last time, I'm not moving in with you." We'd gone back and forth over this since he had found out about the threats.

On the one hand, I liked the idea of staying in his home. I would feel safer there, with him. Except that moving in with him was sure to goad whoever the stalker was into attacking. Not only that, but the lack of privacy came with its own potential issues.

There was no way that I could stay at Patrick's without him realizing that something was going on with me. Without him connecting the dots and realizing that I was pregnant.

Unfortunately, Patrick still wasn't listening to me. He steered me toward the doorway.

"You can't just bully me into doing what you say," I snapped, digging in my heels.

"Where your safety is concerned, Emily, I will be the world's biggest bully," he told me. He refused to listen to any of my other arguments, dragging me to the door. Our security detail trailed after us.

At my parents' condo, Patrick helped me pack a couple bags. "Write a note telling your parents you'll be staying with me for a few days," he coaxed.

"I'm going to tell them that we're on a business trip," I corrected. "They still don't know..." I trailed off, feeling myself blush. I still hadn't told my parents one thing about Patrick and me. But I refused to feel bad about that right now. There was nothing to tell.

I could see Patrick gritting his teeth. Honestly, that made me feel a little better. He was frustrated. Good. I was pretty frustrated as well.

"I don't understand why I can't just stay here, if I've got the security team," I protested as I watched Patrick pack my things.

"This place doesn't have enough space for a 24/7 security team," Patrick said, and I could tell that he was losing his patience. "Besides, I've got a doorman at my building. That's an added layer of protection even when we're not there."

I shook my head. "I still think you're going overboard," I told him. But I had to admit, I kind of liked the fact that he seemed to have thought of everything. It made me feel safer.

In the end, I gave up and followed him back out to the car, and we headed for his place. I was curious to see where he lived when he was in Saratoga, but I wasn't expecting the amazing place that it was. He lived in one of the newer buildings in town, and his penthouse apartment overlooked the rest of Saratoga Springs. The place was gorgeous, and surprisingly huge.

"You know, for a bachelor, this place isn't bad," I told

him. Then I frowned. "Wait, though. You don't own it, do you? You live in Boston."

Patrick shrugged. "Actually, I bought this place back when I was still playing hockey, just to have a place to come home to." He paused and rubbed sheepishly at the back of his neck. "Only then I basically didn't come home at all."

I cocked my head to the side. "Why not?" I asked, wondering if I wanted to know the answer.

Patrick just gave me a look. "Why don't I give you a tour?" he suggested and proceeded to do just that.

"And I guess this would be your bedroom," he finally said, pulling open the door. "I'd feel safer if you shared my bed, though." There was a twinkle in his eye that let me know that he was just kidding, but I rolled my eyes all the same.

"I'll let you bully me this far, but not into your bed," I told him.

Patrick smiled. "Maybe I'll have to try convincing you in other ways," he said.

I was about to ask what those ways were when I was struck by another wave of nausea. I ended up running into the ensuite bathroom and gagging again, leaning miserably against the toilet bowl. Yep, he was definitely going to find out what was going on with me. It was only a matter of time.

# CHAPTER 34

## PATRICK

I listened as Emily heaved into the toilet yet again. I was worried about her. Not only did she have a stalker, but she still seemed to be feeling under the weather, even though she had assured me that she was doing better today.

I called the town doctor without any hesitation. The man promised to be over as soon as possible—one of the perks of having money: doctors who made house calls at a moment's notice.

I then went into the bathroom and helped Emily to her feet. "You should rest," I said, nudging her toward the bed.

She shook her head. "I'm fine," she insisted, much as she had the day before. "I'd love a cup of tea, though, if you have any."

"Sure," I said, "as long as you'll take it easy." I nudged her toward the bed again before heading off to the kitchen.

When I came back, she was hanging her clothes in the closet. I had to smile at the sight. So maybe our marriage was a sham, and maybe she refused to date me, but she was living with me, at least for now. It felt good, whatever the circumstances were that had led us to this point.

My phone rang. It was Jonah, calling to let me know that he had a private investigation team working on the stalker. They wanted access to Emily's phone records, and for that, they needed her permission. I looked over at her. I didn't want to upset her so recently after she'd been sick.

"I'll work on it, okay?" I told Jonah. "I'll get back to you tonight."

"What was that about?" Emily asked as I hung up the phone.

I waved off the question. Fortunately, the doorbell rang just then. The security team was vetting the doctor by the time I reached the hallway, and I smiled. There was no way anyone was getting to Emily with them around.

I showed the doctor to Emily's room and introduced the two of them. Emily looked shocked to see that I had called him. "Patrick, honestly, I'm fine. I don't need an examination."

"Emily, come on," I said exasperatedly. "You can't keep anything down. I'm worried about you. I don't know if this is just stress because of the stalker or what, but I want the doctor to check you out."

"I'm here anyway," Dr. Gilroy added. "I might as well give you a little check-up."

"No," Emily said flatly, folding her arms across her chest.

"She's been throwing up," I said to the doctor. "Every afternoon. Maybe more. And she's been exhausted too. I think she's achy, like with the flu? Or maybe it's cramps, I don't know."

Dr. Gilroy was giving Emily a considering look. Emily, for her part, looked mortified. "Patrick, would you mind giving us a moment alone?" the doctor asked.

I blinked in surprise. I hated the idea of leaving the

room. Emily clearly wasn't going to tell me what was really going on, and I was going to worry until I knew. But finally, I nodded. Outside in the hallway, I shifted from foot to foot, wishing that I could hear what they were talking about.

When the doctor emerged, he was smiling. "She's going to be fine," he said, clapping a hand on my shoulder. "Don't worry." That was it. Then he left.

I gnashed my teeth together. "Emily, so help me God, if you don't tell me what's going on with you—" I started.

"I told you that I'm fine," she argued.

"Obviously you're not," I snapped. "It's not normal to be throwing up food every afternoon, not unless you're sick or..." My words trailed off as suddenly I realized the truth. "Are you pregnant?" I asked incredulously.

Emily froze, staring down at her hands. "What makes you think that?" she asked, and I could tell that she was trying to sound nonchalant, but she looked like she was on the verge of panicking.

I stared at her. Pregnant. Emily was pregnant. A whirlwind of emotions swirled up inside of me. I didn't know how to feel about it.

There was a part of me that was elated. We were having a baby, just like I'd imagined we would all those years ago.

There was a part of me that was confused. We weren't even in a relationship. How were we going to provide the best life possible for this baby if we couldn't even get through a day without fighting at this point?

But the biggest part of me was hurt and upset. Emily had told me that she wouldn't want to build our relationship on lies, but she had evidently known about this for some time now and she hadn't told me. I couldn't help feeling betrayed.

# CHAPTER 35

## EMILY

I didn't know what I expected Patrick's reaction to be when I told him about the baby, but it wasn't this. He just went so silent. Sure, I knew that there were complications there, and things that we were going to need to talk about.

I hadn't wanted him to find out this way. I still had barely had a chance to think things through for myself. This baby was totally unexpected, and even though I knew that it had been conceived during an act of love, no doubt on the night of our fake wedding, and even though I knew that it was Patrick's baby, I just didn't know what to do about it.

I had barely had time to think about the situation given everything with Patrick and then this stalker.

Now he knew, though. The question was, what would he do with that information?

Nothing, it seemed. Instead, he just stared at me, looking shell-shocked. I couldn't read the emotions that flickered across his face; they were gone too quickly. Was he happy? Worried? Angry?

I probably deserved anger most of all. I hadn't told him

about it. I should have told him right when I first found out. I'd just been so scared.

"Patrick," I started to say, but he shook his head.

"You should have told me," he said accusingly.

"I just found out recently," I sighed. "I was going to tell you, I just hadn't found the right moment."

Patrick stared at me for a long moment, but I could see that that, at least, he believed me. "Okay," he said. "So—"

"Can we talk about this tomorrow?" I found myself pleading. "There's no rush. I'm not that far along. I just don't want either of us to say anything that we might regret."

Patrick slowly nodded. "Fine," he said.

"I really want to get a little rest," I added, hoping that he would get the hint and leave. All the excitement from the day had left me feeling drained. More than that, I just wanted a little space. I was worried that even if I told Patrick I didn't want to talk about this now, he was going to try to talk about it anyway. After all, he seemed to think he ruled my life at the moment.

The next morning, things seemed blissfully normal. I woke up to the sounds of Patrick singing along to the radio, and when I padded out to the kitchen, he had waffles ready to go. "Morning," he said, smiling his trademark crooked smile at me. "I didn't know if you were headed into work today, but I figured I could at least make you some breakfast before I go. There's a fresh pot of tea, too."

"Thanks," I said, sitting down at the table and helping myself to tea. I had to admit, it was nice to feel so pampered and taken care of by Patrick. It felt like I was getting a glimpse into how things could be if we really were in a relationship. And I sort of liked it.

It made me wonder about the future. One of the main

reasons against starting a relationship with him now was gone; he knew about the pregnancy. Hopefully, the stalker would be taken care of soon and then we could figure out what exactly we were going to do.

As one by one my excuses slipped away, I started to wonder if maybe, just maybe, Patrick and I could actually have a relationship someday. Was that what I wanted for the future? Patrick and I, our baby, a family? It might just be, if I let myself dare to believe that it could happen. Patrick and I would get married for real, in the ceremony that I had always imagined.

That was far in the future for now, though.

We headed in to work together. "Aren't you worried that someone might see us together?" I asked Patrick.

"We've got the security team with us," he reminded me. "And besides, it's about time that everyone in the office knew about this anyway." He paused. "I know you're worried that one of them might be the stalker, but I'm wondering if maybe it's better for us to be upfront about our relationship. Maybe the stalker will realize that they have no chance, or maybe they'll make a move and we'll figure out exactly who it was. For the record, I don't think it's anyone in the company."

I sighed. "All right," I finally agreed, mainly because I could tell that there was no sense in arguing with him.

We walked in together, and no one so much as shot a second glance toward us. When I really thought about it, I supposed everyone had probably already learned about the two of us the day before. We hadn't exactly been subtle, especially not leaving with the security detail in tow.

Still, it was a surprise when Patrick pulled me into a quick hug as I made to get off the elevator. "I'll see you this afternoon," he promised me.

I nodded and headed for my office. I had just gotten there when I got a text from Alyssa. *You're missing again! Went to your place and you weren't there.*

I stared down at my phone, wondering if I really wanted to have this conversation with her right now. I was tired, and I just wanted things to be normal again, somehow. Then again, she knew that I was pregnant. Maybe she could help me come up with some kind of way to talk to Patrick about it.

I dialed Alyssa's number. "Hey!" she said brightly when I answered. "Where are you, anyway?"

"Right now, I'm at work," I told her. I took a deep breath. "The reason that I wasn't around last night is because I've moved in with Patrick." I found myself grinning as I said it. "Actually, there's a lot to catch you up on."

"Why don't we meet for lunch?" Alyssa suggested.

"Sounds perfect," I agreed.

I wasn't thrilled to have the security team tag along with me to the restaurant, and Alyssa was surprised to see them. I sighed as I dropped into a seat across from her. "So apparently I have a stalker," I told her. "They've been sending me threats telling me to stay away from Patrick. Sorry I didn't tell you sooner, I just didn't know how to even handle it."

Alyssa looked shocked. "That's terrible," she said. "Why would you move in with Patrick if you're that worried, though? Sounds like the last place you'd want to be."

"He didn't give me a choice, really," I told her, shrugging. "And I doubt he'll let me leave now. Obviously my symptoms were really visible once I was living with him, so it didn't take long for him to realize that I'm pregnant."

"What did he say to that?" Alyssa asked, and I could see a certain sharpness of worry in her eyes.

I shook my head. "We haven't talked about it yet. I wanted both of us to have a chance to think about it before we talked."

Alyssa nodded. Just then, our food was delivered to the table. I got one good whiff of whatever she had ordered and thought I was going to hurl. "I'll be right back," I muttered, making a beeline for the bathroom.

"I'll come with you," Alyssa said, following me. "I'll hold your hair back. That's what friends are for, right?"

I didn't manage to bring up much since I hadn't eaten since breakfast, but I still felt drained as Alyssa reached over to flush the toilet. "Thanks," I sighed, getting to my feet. I pushed the stall door open and froze.

Standing there in the middle of the bathroom was a large man dressed in all dark clothes, with a facemask pulled down over his head. I started to freak out, but I barely had a chance to do that before he had thrown a cloth filled with some foul-smelling substance over my mouth.

I struggled for just a moment before everything went black.

# CHAPTER 36

## PATRICK

I was in the middle of a meeting when my phone started ringing. One glance at the screen showed me that this couldn't wait. It was one of the security guys. "Emily is missing," he said, with no preamble.

I froze, my blood turning to ice in my veins. "What do you mean she's missing?" I asked, barely managing to control my temper. This was one of the best security crews that Jonah had been able to find in our area. And not even one day had gone by before they lost her.

What the fuck happened?" I snarled.

"She went out to lunch with a friend," the man explained. "They went into the bathroom together. Emily was feeling sick. Then the next thing we knew, the friend stumbled out of there maybe ten minutes later, and she was pretty groggy and confused. Emily was gone."

I swore explosively. "How?" I asked, beginning to pace agitatedly. I didn't care who in the office saw me right now; my only concern was for Emily.

"The friend said that there was a man in the bathroom,

dressed all in black and wearing a ski mask or something," the security man told me. "She's not so sure what happened, she thought she might have been drugged but when she came to, the man and Emily were both gone."

I clenched my phone hard enough that I could hear the plastic creaking beneath my fingers. I wanted to rage at the man for incompetence. Shouldn't they have a female guard with the crew to make sure that shit like this didn't happen?

I knew that there were dozens of ways that the security crew could have been avoided though. I knew that they had done their best.

There was no way in hell that I was going to let anything happen to Emily.

"Bring her friend here," I growled, hanging up on the man. Then I stalked off to find Jonah. "Tell the PI to break into Emily's phone if he has to," I told him. "She's missing, and we've got to find her immediately."

Jonah nodded, looking worried. "On it," he promised me, squeezing my shoulder as he passed me. I could barely feel the touch. Comfort had no place in my world at the moment.

The security team finally arrived. I was surprised to see that Alyssa was who she'd been at lunch with, although I don't know why. After all, I knew that the two of them were friends. Suddenly, though, all I could think about was the fact that Emily was being threatened by someone who didn't want her anywhere near me, and Alyssa had always been rather forceful about the crush she had on me.

No. Alyssa couldn't be the stalker. She would have made a move like this years ago if she were that crazy and interested in me. Besides, she wouldn't have attacked herself in the bathroom just for the sake of making Emily disappear. Not only that, but the two of them were good friends, and Emily was smart enough that she would have realized if Alyssa was lying to her. Right?

Alyssa fell into my arms, weeping dramatically. "Oh Patrick, it was so horrible," she said.

"What happened?" I asked tersely. I wanted to dump her out of my arms, I wanted to run to wherever it was that Emily was and comfort her instead. But I forced myself to hold on to Alyssa and absently pat her back.

"I'm so sorry!" Alyssa sobbed. "I failed you, and I failed Emily. I don't even know what happened, just one minute we were in the bathroom and she was getting sick, and the next moment I was stumbling out of there and the security guys were all over me."

"So you don't remember anything that happened in the bathroom?" I asked sharply. The security guard had said that she remembered a man in all black and a facemask of some kind.

"Not much," Alyssa said, gingerly touching the back of her skull. "I must have hit my head when I fell." She paused and squinted like she was thinking really hard. "There was a man there, and he had some sort of cloth. It smelled really bad. That's all I remember. I must have passed out."

"Chloroform or something like it," one of the security guards said. "We've got guys still at the scene who are talking with the authorities."

I nodded distractedly. Alyssa's fingernails were digging into my arm, as though she was desperate to draw my attention back to her. "I just can't believe this is happening," she said tearfully. "My best friend has been taken away from me, and there's nothing that I can do about it."

I wanted to slap her. She was acting as though she was

the only person concerned about Emily. She had to realize how much I cared about the woman. *Especially since she's pregnant with my child.* I wondered if Alyssa knew that part.

Jonah suddenly appeared, a grim grin on his face. "Well, we've managed to track her down," he said.

"Already?" I asked in surprise. I was of course glad to hear it, but I was a bit shocked that she could be found so quickly.

"Whatever idiot it was that kidnapped her, they weren't smart enough to ditch her phone, apparently," Jonah explained. "We've got a GPS signal."

"Where?" I asked immediately. I didn't know what I could do to help the situation, but I knew that I had to try. Maybe I could reason with the stalker. After all, they were clearly interested in me, not Emily. They were just using Emily to get to me.

Whatever it was that they wanted, I was prepared to give them. Money, anything. I didn't care. I just wanted Emily safely back in my arms.

"If you're coming, let's go," one of the security guys said to me, cocking his head toward the door.

"You can't leave me here!" Alyssa said, holding tighter to me.

"Alyssa, I have to go make sure that Emily is okay," I said impatiently.

"What if that man comes back, looking for me this time?" Alyssa all but wailed.

I gently but firmly pried her hands off from my arm. "Alyssa, I'm pretty sure if that man had wanted you, he would already have you," I pointed out. "Anyway, how would he know that you were here? I don't know why they took Emily, maybe something to do with her father's debts, but I'm sure it has nothing to do with you or this company. You'll be safe here."

Unless those warning bells in the back of my head were there for a reason, along with that niggling worry that something about her story just wasn't right.

# CHAPTER 37

## EMILY

I woke up tied to a chair. My heart was beating a mile a minute, and I could barely figure out what the heck had happened. The last thing I remembered was lunch with Alyssa. How had I ended up here? My head was throbbing, but finally I remembered. The man in the bathroom. I didn't know what he had done to me, but I could feel my stomach churn, and my head would not stop pounding.

The baby. Would whatever the guy had used on me hurt the baby?

What was he going to do to me?

I couldn't even see where I was. They had me blindfolded, my hands and feet tightly bound so that I could barely move. I started crying, unable to help it. What was going to happen to me?

I could hear someone moving, although I couldn't make out what they were doing. "Please," I said, my voice ragged with tears. "Please, don't hurt me. You have to let me go."

No response.

"Please, I didn't mean to do anything wrong," I tried

again. "Patrick and I are just old friends. That's it. We aren't together or anything like that."

Still nothing. I shivered, huddling over as much as I could. It made my shoulders hurt, but then again, everything ached at the moment. "What are you going to do to me?" I asked, my voice barely above a whisper. Unsurprisingly, there was no response.

I shivered there in the chair, getting more and more anxious. I knew that someone must know that I was missing by now. The security team would be worried when I didn't come back. But would they be able to find me? Where was I? My thoughts chased around and around in my head.

Most of all, besides my panic, I felt guilty. If this was the end, there were so many things that I wished that I had said to Patrick first. I wished that I had told him that I loved him. I wished that we had talked about the baby. I wished that I had told him the real reason I broke up with him so many years ago now, the reasons that I could never forget him or move on from him.

I felt like I had wasted all my chances with him.

In a different lifetime, if I had just opened my eyes a little sooner, what could we have had? What had I missed out on? In my heart, I knew the answer all too well. I had been dreaming about a life with Patrick since high school. I knew exactly what I was missing.

I sobbed, hearing my attacker come closer. They started to speak in that same mechanical voice that I had heard over the phone. "You haven't been listening to me. I told you that you needed to stay away from Patrick Manning. You didn't." There was a pause. "This time, I'm going to make sure that you do."

I trembled, fear overcoming my whole body. "Please," I

whispered. "Please, please, don't hurt me. I didn't mean to. I won't go near him again. I promise."

I hated the thought of losing Patrick from my life, but if that's what it took to guarantee the safety of our baby, then that was what I was going to have to do. The footsteps were getting closer, showing no sign of stopping.

"Please," I begged one final time. "Please, I'm pregnant. Just whatever you do, don't hurt my baby. Please."

Suddenly, I heard something drop to the floor with a loud crash. The next thing I knew, the blindfold was being torn off me. Elliot stood there, looking as though he had seen a ghost. I was sure I didn't look much better.

My eyes fell to the floor. A voice distorter. *Elliot* was the stalker?

"Emily, I'm so sorry," he said, his face flushing bright red. "I knew that I never should have gone along with Alyssa's plans, but I just couldn't help myself. I've been in love with her for so long, I'll do anything she wants just to make her happy." He shifted back and forth, looking like he didn't know what to do now.

He paused, but I still couldn't find my voice as I tried to parse what he was saying. Elliot? Seriously?

"This was my only way to be close to her," he whispered. "You have to know what it feels like to love someone so much that you'll do anything to be with them."

I nodded slowly. I looked around, trying to calm myself down. Suddenly, I recognized where we were. "Is this my old house?" I asked in shock.

"No one's bought it yet, if that's what you're wondering," Elliot said defensively. "It was the perfect place to hide you. No one is going to disturb us. We're not trespassing."

"Why?" I finally asked. "Not you, but Alyssa. Why?" I

had thought that Alyssa was my best friend. Why would she have wanted to scare me so badly?

"You know that," Elliot said, sounding miserable. "Alyssa wants Patrick for herself. She's always hated you for drawing his attention away from her."

"She's my best friend," I whispered. "She doesn't hate me. Does she?"

Elliot gave me a look that was almost sympathetic. I swallowed hard.

"The best way she could think to get you to leave him alone was to scare you until you weren't a problem anymore," Elliot added.

"What were you going to do to me?" I asked slowly, even though I wasn't sure that I really wanted to know. I could imagine all the different sorts of torture that he might use. But when I looked around, I saw that he didn't even have any sort of weapon. Nothing beyond a voice distortion device. Maybe he really had just wanted to scare me.

"Nothing," Elliot said quickly. "Seriously, I swear, I wasn't going to do anything. Alyssa just told me to kidnap you and then scare you a little. I would never have actually hurt you." He paused, grimacing. "She didn't tell me that you were pregnant though." He shook his head. "Things have gone too far. They have to end now. I'm sorry that I ever helped Alyssa do this horrible thing."

I sighed and shook my head. "Just untie me, Elliot."

He jumped into action, looking horrified that he hadn't started doing that right away. "So you're really pregnant, huh?" he asked quietly as he untied my wrists. "Or was that just a line to get me to stop?"

"I'm really pregnant," I sighed.

"Is it Patrick's?" Elliot asked, and I could hear the hope in his voice.

Poor guy. He probably thought that a pregnancy would make Alyssa give up her crush on Patrick once and for all. Instead, it seemed to have only made her crazier.

"Elliot, you can do so much better than Alyssa," I said, even though I could tell he already knew that.

He didn't respond, but that was probably for the best.

I still couldn't get over the fact that Alyssa had been the stalker the whole time, and that she had dragged Elliot into this. She had been my friend. They had both been my friends. Had Alyssa been pretending for all this time, ever since we were in high school? I couldn't believe it.

Then again, I knew that I used to not be a particularly nice girl. To Alyssa, this was probably just some harmless prank. She just wanted to scare me so that she could get what she wanted. She was only thinking about herself. Just like I had been when I'd broken Patrick's heart all those years ago.

I shook my head. Before I could think about it any longer, though, the door burst open and Patrick flew inside with the security team. They threw Elliot to the ground, training guns on him.

"Stop!" I cried. "Don't hurt him. Please!"

Maybe I shouldn't be sticking up for Elliot, but I knew in my heart that he wasn't a bad guy. He just loved Alyssa too much, and he'd spent twelve years or however long trying to get her to notice him.

He wasn't the mastermind behind this. Sure, he should have to face some consequences for his actions, but he wasn't dangerous. He was just a man in love.

"What the hell is going on?" Patrick growled, looking like he wished he had a gun that he himself could pull on Elliot. Finally, he dragged his gaze away from the man and looked at me. "Emily, are you all right?"

"I'm okay," I assured him. "Elliot kidnapped me, but he wasn't working alone. I mean, look around. He doesn't have weapons or anything. He wasn't actually going to hurt me. They were just trying to scare me."

"Who is they?" Patrick asked slowly, but from the expression on his face, I could tell that he already had a hunch.

"It was Alyssa," I told him, clinging to his arm. "Alyssa was behind this whole thing. She's wanted you ever since high school, and she figured if she could scare me enough, then it would give her a chance with you finally."

Patrick stared blankly at me. Then, he whistled under his breath. "Alyssa?" he asked. "I knew her story sounded weird. She's in my office right now. She came there the second you were kidnapped, crying and trying to make it all about her." He sounded disgusted as he ran a hand back through his hair. "And Elliot?"

I glanced down at him. Elliot had been my friend too. We might not have been as close as Alyssa and I were, but I still couldn't believe he had agreed to kidnap me. Then again, we all did crazy things when we were in love.

*Like breaking up with a man you love and refusing to see or hear from him for the next decade,* I thought ruefully.

I had certainly made my own mistakes in life. This was Elliot's.

I turned to Patrick. "He was only doing what Alyssa wanted him to do. He loves her, and he just wanted to make her happy."

Patrick shook his head. "Pretty shitty thing to agree to," he spat.

"Don't I know it," Elliot muttered from the floor, and Patrick's lips twitched into the faintest of smiles. He nodded at the guards and then turned to me.

"The police should be here soon. They'll need to question you, but in light of your injuries, we're going to take you to a doctor first." I started to protest, but that stopped when he scooped me up into his arms and carried me out of the house. He placed me gently into an SUV and gave the driver directions to his apartment.

"I already called the doctor. He's going to meet us there," Patrick informed me as he climbed in beside me. "I thought you might prefer to do the police interview there, too. I think you can do that. If not, I'll donate a new training facility or something, whatever it takes. I don't want you to have to go through anything else."

I rolled my eyes. "Patrick, seriously. I'm fine," I told him. Then I frowned, my hand dropping to my belly. I knew that was what he was really worried of; that somehow, this ordeal had hurt the baby. "You're right," I said softly, even though I was sure that there was nothing wrong with either of us. "We should get checked out. Just to make sure."

Patrick flashed me a dazzling smile.

"So what happens now?" I asked.

"With us or with Alyssa?" Patrick asked.

"Both, I guess."

"As for Alyssa, and Elliot as well, that's up to the authorities to figure out," Patrick said. He leaned in closer, his lips brushing the shell of my ear. "As for us, I guess that remains to be seen."

From the way he said it, though, and the shiver that ran down my spine, I knew that we were both on the same page. We knew exactly what was coming next. And we were both looking forward to it.

# CHAPTER 38

## PATRICK

I could barely believe what had just happened. Emily had been kidnapped and tied up. By Elliot, of all people. We would get to that one later. But for now, I was still trying to process the fact that Emily had been kidnapped.

It was as though my body refused to accept the fact that she was safe now; that she was right there next to me. It had been difficult enough to accept the truth when the PI told us where the GPS signal from Emily's phone was coming from.

Her parents' old mansion.

I had never been so far into the old house before. Emily hadn't wanted me there when we were teenagers, sure that her parents wouldn't accept me. After all, she was a rich girl, and I was just some average boy. They wanted better for their daughter.

That all seemed so trivial now. If that was the reason she had broken up with me, then so be it. But I wasn't going to spend the next ten years, or the rest of my life, dwelling on it.

In fact, I felt stupid now for all the time that I had wasted. All those years when I hadn't seen her. I had professed my love to her, but then I had just let her walk away. Sure, I had been hurt, and sure, she had had other plans for herself. But I could have fought harder to keep her. I never should have let her go.

It was what Jonah had told me when I was trying to figure out what to do after the disastrous joke wedding. He told me to woo her, to be persistent. It was how I had gotten her in the first place. Maybe that was what relationships were. You just had to keep fighting.

I hadn't done that, and that's how I had lost Emily before.

This time, I had vowed to fight.

I reached over, brushing my fingers across the back of her hand. She was still there. Good.

I called Jonah as we sped off to my place, confirming that Alyssa was still there and telling him to make sure that she stayed there until the authorities arrived. What an idiot. Did she think that we really wouldn't be able to trace this all back to her?

Of course, none of it seemed to have been too well thought out. I was only glad that things hadn't gone any farther. Who knew what they might have done to Emily, accidentally or otherwise?

"I'll fill you in on everything later," I assured Jonah. "But right now, my number one priority is Emily."

"Of course," Jonah said immediately.

She had been my number one priority ever since I found out that she was in trouble. Well, to be honest, Emily had been my number one priority for a lot longer than that. The thing was, I couldn't imagine my life without her. I had already had to spend a decade without her, and that had nearly killed me. I knew that I couldn't lose her again.

I reached over and pulled her a little closer to me, still trying to reassure myself that she was okay, that she was actually here, by my side.

"You're sure you're okay?" I asked Emily when I got off the phone.

She smiled at me. "Exhausted," she admitted, snuggling into my side. "But I'm okay. The baby is too, I'm sure of it." She smiled. "I'm not that far along yet, but I feel like I already have the motherly instinct that everyone always talks about. After a certain point, I didn't care what Elliot was going to do to me, as long as he didn't hurt our baby. We're both fine."

"Good," I sighed, stroking her hair. I couldn't bear to think about either of them getting hurt through this. All because some crazy lady had a crush on me. Some crazy lady that I definitely didn't care about, whom I had never led on in any way. "Emily, if anyone hurt you, I don't know what I would do."

Emily leaned over and kissed me gently. "I'm glad we didn't have to find out," she said softly. "I'm glad that everything worked out okay."

I squeezed her hand, thinking about that. Things really had worked out okay, somehow. I still wasn't sure how it had turned around so quickly for us. One minute we were fighting and the next minute, there we were, wrapped in each other's arms.

I supposed that was sort of the way that our whole relationship had gone, up to and including Emily breaking up with me. One minute, things were going well, and the next minute, she was walking away, not to be seen for another ten years.

Once, that would have scared me. What if I lost her again? What if she decided to leave? But I was starting to realize that in spite everything, Emily really did love me just like she had told me. I still didn't know what exactly made the switch flip on our relationship, but I was going to keep fighting for her until I figured it out and ensured that I never had to watch her walk away.

"Are you sure going home like this is allowed?" Emily asked suddenly. "Won't the police want me to go to the station or something to give my statement?"

"I don't really give a fuck if this is allowed or not; it's what's happening," I told her. I turned to her, cupping her cheeks in my palms. "I thought I might have lost you," I said, my voice choked with tears.

She leaned in and kissed me gently, with all the compassion in the world. "But you didn't," she reminded me softly.

When we reached my home, I carried her up and into the bedroom and laid her down gently. Dr. Gilroy did a basic checkup, including the use of a handheld ultrasound, and announced that everything was going to be fine. Finally, I felt some of the tension drain out of me.

After the doctor left, I crawled onto the bed with Emily, pulling her into my arms and holding her. "I was so terrified of losing you," I told her in a whisper. "When they told me that you were missing, it was like I went totally crazy. I was willing to anything to make sure you and our baby came back to me safely."

I put my hand on her stomach, knowing that the life we had created lay just beneath my palm. It was a powerful feeling.

"You know, the whole time I was sitting there tied to that chair, all I could think about, other than my panic of course, was all the things that I should have said to you," Emily sighed.

"Such as?" I asked, wanting to hear her actually say the words.

Emily propped herself up on one elbow, looking down at me. "You know, I never thought that I was better than you." She put a finger over my lips when I started to interrupt her. "No, listen to me. I know I said that we were from two different worlds and that it couldn't work out, but that was just the best excuse I could give you. One where you would never want me again."

"What do you mean?" I asked.

Emily sighed and stared down at the bedding. "I was scared," she admitted. "You had all these plans for our lives, ideas for where we were going to live and, well, everything. And I was scared. We were so young. I had nothing to bring to the relationship, either. I needed to figure out who I was, so that I could be better for you. That's all that Europe was about."

"Then why did you cut me out of your life after that?" I asked quietly.

"Because I was scared that you might not want me back," Emily said, a couple tears slipping down her cheeks. "I was scared that I was going to have to watch you find someone else who would never treat you the way that I had. That you were going to start making future plans with her."

I pulled her close to me again, kissing her as gently as I possibly could. "Never," I said succinctly.

"Never?" she asked.

"Never," I repeated. "Emily, I love you. I've always loved you. And now that you're back in my life, I'm never letting you go."

Emily stared down at me, hope in her gaze. Then, slowly, she smiled, her lips curving perfectly.

I matched her lips with my own, kissing her until she was breathless. She was all right, and somehow, *we* were going to be all right.

I kissed her again.

# CHAPTER 39

## EMILY

As Patrick made love to me, I could tell just how worried he had been for me. He had never stared down at me with this intensity before. He had never kissed me like this before. The adrenaline had left my system, but I still felt like I couldn't get enough of him. I couldn't help thinking about all those things that I had wanted to say to him, if that had really been the end.

I had said some but not all of it already. But the rest I could say without words.

Patrick carefully removed my clothing, kissing his way along my skin as he did so. I couldn't help but giggle. "How awkward would it be if the police showed up looking for a statement right now?" I asked.

Patrick rolled his eyes. "Is that what you're thinking about?" he asked, but before I could answer, he plunged his fingers inside of me, and *oh,* suddenly I wasn't thinking about much of anything at all except for the delicious sensation of his digits buried deep inside my cavern.

His other fingers trailed down my body, followed by his eyes, like he was trying to memorize every inch of me. I shivered under his gaze, and he looked up at me, his dark eyes heavy with the weight of his desire. He slowly bent down to kiss me, even as he crooked his fingers inside of me and worked me open.

My body was aching for him to hurry, to bring me to the brink and let me spill over into pleasure. But my soul needed him to take his time like this. I stroked my fingers down his body as well, feeling every divot and every crevasse, every muscle and every inch of smooth, soft skin. I knew that I would never forget the way we moved together; it was ingrained in my memories and had been since we were teens.

This was something special, though. It felt like giving myself to him all over again. Only this time, it wasn't my virginity. This time, it was my whole life. This time, it was everything.

I trembled as my heart soared with love. Patrick smiled down at me like he knew just how I felt. He pushed into me slowly but surely and then paused, staring down at me. Again, it was as though we were both trying to memorize the moment. I couldn't imagine anyone else ever fitting so perfectly inside of me or against me.

I put my hands on Patrick's hips, guiding his movements, moving my own body against his. We started off slow and languid, like we had all the time in the world, which it finally felt like we did.

He began to pick up the pace, and I snapped my hips up to meet his, feeling the pulse of him deep inside my core. He nibbled at my neck, no doubt leaving a mark there, but I didn't care. I was his, and no one else was ever going to mess with me again.

I gasped as he shifted, the angle causing the head of his cock to drag along my walls with each new thrust. One of his hands toyed with my breasts; the other fell down between my legs, playing absently with my clit as he continued to pound into me.

I felt as though I could barely hold on to my sense of being, as though I was one giant nerve just pulsing with heat. I stopped trying to fight the sensation and gave myself over to it, screaming out Patrick's name as we twisted together, joined together forever, just the two of us.

*The three of us,* I suddenly realized. Patrick and I, and our little baby as well. Still just a seed, the promise of a wonderful future.

I smiled as I relaxed back against the sheets. Patrick thrust deeply one more time and emptied himself into me on a growl. As he fell to the side, I hummed happily, unable to even open my eyes with how well-fucked I was.

"Oh, don't go to sleep yet," Patrick warned. "We're not done."

I shivered with anticipation and turned back to face him. "Good," I said, and he laughed, pulling me into his arms.

Afterward, as we lay there staring at the ceiling, Patrick's arms wrapped around me, I couldn't help thinking about how different things were now than they had been back when we were still just kids. It wasn't just that we were more mature, or that he had money now and I didn't. It wasn't that I had found a career. But somehow, I did have more to bring to this relationship, and so did he.

Not only that, but my feelings were so much stronger than they used to be. I had always loved him, at least in the high school crush version of love. But what I felt for him now couldn't compare at all. It was so much more powerful, and it would be impossible to walk away from.

I leaned over and nuzzled his neck. Patrick smiled as he

kissed my forehead and put a hand back on my stomach. "I love you," I murmured, watching his expression. Sure enough, his whole face lit up in that way that was distinctly his.

"I've loved you since I first saw you," he retorted, leaning down to kiss me. This time, it was slow and sultry. I could feel my body stir to passion again. Already. I blushed, and Patrick laughed knowingly.

"Are you sure you're okay with the fact that I'm pregnant?" I couldn't help asking.

Patrick propped himself up on his elbows so that he was looking down at me. "I can't say that I planned to knock you up so soon, but then again, at least we're not still in high school anymore."

I laughed. "Amen," I said. "My parents would have killed you."

"But I can't wait to raise a family with you now," Patrick continued. "You're going to make an amazing mother. I just know it."

"I'm sorry I was such an idiot before," I told him.

"There's only one way to make it up to me," Patrick told me seriously. He leaned over me and pulled a small box from the drawer of his nightstand. He opened it to reveal an intricate, rose gold ring with diamonds sparkling from every side of it. "Marry me? For real this time."

I was stunned. "Pat," I said, sitting up. "When did you...?"

"Pretty much the second we got back from Niagara Falls," he admitted. "I had hoped that I would go see my lawyer and she would assure me that we were legitimately married. And then I would offer you the choice of remaining my wife. Only then I found out about this stupid thing called a marriage license."

He grinned crookedly at me, but I was as far from laughing as could be.

"Emily Andrews, will you give me another chance? I want nothing more than to spend the rest of my life making you happy and providing for our little family," he said.

I smiled and kissed him. "Yes," I said, tears clumping my eyelashes. "Yes, Pat. Yes." I paused. "But on one condition." I watched Pat's face fall. "Santa can't sing at our wedding," I finished.

He laughed and shook his head. "It's a deal," he said.

"So I guess I need to tell my parents about you now, huh?" I asked as Patrick slipped the ring on my finger.

He grinned. "Well, it depends, I guess," he said. "Are we getting an annulment this time or not?"

"Never," I growled, wrapping a hand around the back of his neck and pulling him in for a fierce kiss. I never wanted to let him go again. And finally, I didn't have to.

# EPILOGUE

## EMILY - ONE YEAR LATER

I took a deep breath, my heart beating a million miles a minute. I couldn't believe that it was about to happen, for real this time. I was about to become Mrs. Patrick Manning. I was about to promise the rest of my life to my best friend.

"Gosh, this dress is beautiful," Mom said, wiping tears from her eyes as she gave me a once-over. But this time, they were happy tears. She and Dad finally seemed settled in their new home and their new lifestyle. I was glad to see that.

I smoothed my hands down along my gown. "One of a kind," I said. I had designed it myself, and I felt like a fairy-tale princess about to go marry her knight in shining armor. I couldn't be happier.

"I still don't really understand why you were so determined to put some of the material from your prom dress in there, but it looks very pretty," Mom added.

I fingered one of the tiny red bows that adorned the sleeves. If she only knew.

She and Dad had finally met Patrick at an end-ofsummer barbecue, but I had decided it wasn't worth trying to explain to them that we had been high school sweethearts once upon a time. Let them think that we had just gone to school together and then reconnected by accidental happenstance.

Patrick had agreed that it was better that way. *"I don't want to lie to them, but I also don't want them to think of me as the guy you were lying about for all those years."*

He had a point.

It had been important to me to include some of the prom dress material in my wedding dress. After all, that red fabric had brought us together on an unforgettable night in high school, and then it had brought us together again when I had sewn it into that jockey uniform so that I could make the pieces fit Patrick's broad shoulders and muscular thighs.

If I were the type to believe in magic, I would definitely have said there was a little magic in that material. Hopefully it would bring us good luck in the future.

Not that we needed luck. I was already marrying my best friend, and we had one beautiful little daughter together. Aimee was sitting with her godfather Jonah and his girlfriend Hanna at the moment, but I couldn't wait to hold her in my arms once the official part of the ceremony was over.

"Well, I'd better go take my seat before it starts," Mom said, winking at me. "Don't want to upstage the bride on her walk down the aisle. Not that I could. You look absolutely stunning."

I laughed. "Thanks, Mom," I said, giving her a quick hug. She hurried down the aisle as Dad came to stand at my side.

"Ready?" he asked quietly.

I beamed, unable to help it. "Yeah," I said. "I'm ready."

The wedding march started, and he walked me slowly down the aisle.

As we waited for the music to end, Patrick leaned in to me. "You know, I thought about dressing up as a jockey, just for a joke," he muttered under his breath. "But we saw how joke weddings go."

"You did get the marriage license this time, didn't you?" I asked, suddenly worried.

Patrick stifled a laugh. "Yes, I got the marriage license," he promised me. "What did I tell you before? Once you came back in my life, I knew that I was never letting you go again. I mean that."

"Good," I said.

The pastor began the ceremony. Just out of spite, and to confuse our guests, I said exactly the same vows as I had last time: "I promise to spend all your money and sew you whatever crazy outfits you want."

Patrick shook his head, a grin on his face. "And I promise you that for better or for worse, in sickness and in health, things are never going to change. I'll always love you."

Afterward, we headed to the reception. "Have I mentioned how beautiful you look today?" Patrick asked as I accepted Aimee back from her godfather.

"You look quite dashing yourself," I said, grinning at him. "It's way better than what you wore for our first wedding."

"I don't even remember what I was wearing," Patrick said, shaking his head.

"I'm pretty sure it was jeans and a flannel," I said.

"Well, you were in a mini-dress," Patrick reminded me, and we both laughed. "Seriously, any regrets?" He actually sounded worried.

I reached over and placed my hand over his on the table. "Pat, look at this place. Everything's perfect. All our favorite people are here. Aimee's been so happy. I've never been this lucky. No regrets."

"Hold on to that feeling," Patrick said, leaning over to kiss my cheek and then suddenly getting up to leave. I frowned, wondering what he was up to, but I didn't have to wonder for long.

Suddenly, the lights lowered, and a man walked onto the stage. It was the dude that looked like Santa from the wedding chapel in Niagara Falls. I didn't know whether to laugh or cry when Patrick came back over to me. I handed Aimee off to Mom as I got to my feet so we could dance.

"I asked you for one thing!" I told him.

"I thought you had gotten used to the fact that I'm going to plan our future however I want to," Patrick said, a twinkle in his eye. "Anyway, it only seemed fitting. I'm not sure we would be here if it wasn't for that whole fiasco."

I mused on that while we danced around the room.

"You may be right," I finally agreed. I grinned. "Anyway, it was my idea to invite Barry and Margaret, so I guess it was only right to invite Santa too."

We spun around, swaying to the song. I felt like I was floating in his arms. Everything was perfect, and I was so glad for everything that had brought us to this point.

"I'm sorry again for being a spoiled little rich girl in high school and breaking up with you," I murmured later that night as we leaned in to cut the cake.

Patrick laughed and kissed my cheek. "At least I have you now," he said. "Anyway, the tables have turned. I'm rich now, and I plan to spoil you and our daughter like crazy. Let's raise a brat who knows what she wants out of life and won't compromise."

I laughed. "Deal," I agreed.

We cut into the cake and shared the first piece, feeding it to one another with our fingers. I dabbed a blot of frosting on Patrick's nose, and the photographer timed the image just right as Patrick went cross-eyed and stuck out his tongue like he was trying to lick it off himself.

As Mom handed Aimee back to me, I had to admit; life had never been sweeter. I couldn't help feeling glad that life had given me a second chance at true love.

THE END

Printed in Great Britain
by Amazon

42996559R00130